Gatherings Volume 13
The En'owkin Journal of
First North American Peoples

Reconciliation
Elders as Knowledge Keepers

Fall 2002

Editors: Leanne Flett Kruger
and Bernelda Wheeler

With special guest foreword
by Leonard Peltier

Theytus Books Ltd.
Penticton, BC

Gatherings
The En'owkin Journal of First North American Peoples Volume 13
2002

National Library of Canada Cataloguing in Publication Data

Main entry under title:

Gatherings

Annual.
ISSN 1180-0666
ISBN 1-894778-06-5 (v. 13)

1. Canadian literature (English)--Indian authors--Periodicals.* 2.
Canadian literature (English)--Periodicals.* 3. American literature--Indian
authors-- Periodicals. 4. American literature--Periodicals. I. En'owkin
International School of Writing. II. En'owkin Centre.
PS8235.I6G35   C810.8'0897   CS91-031483-7
PR9194.5.I5G35

Editorial Committee: Leanne Flett Kruger and
Bernelda Wheeler
Cover Painting: Julie Flett
Layout and Design: Leanne Flett Kruger
Proofing: Chick Gabriel, Audrey Huntley and Greg Young-Ing

Please send submissions and letters to
Gatherings,
En'owkin Centre, R.R.#2, Site 50, Comp. 8, V2A 6J7, Canada.
Previously published works are not considered.

*The publisher acknowledges the support of the Canada Council for the Arts, the
Department of Canadian Heritage and the British Columbia Arts Council in
publication of this book.*

BRITISH
COLUMBIA
ARTS COUNCIL

Canadä

The Canada Council
Conseil des Arts du Canada

Gatherings
Volume 13

Reconciliation
Elders as Knowledge Keepers

Table of Contents

First Words

Section 1 – Lessons

Section 2 – Gifts

Section 3 – Knowledge

Section 4 – Honouring

Section 5 – International and Words from our Youth

Biographies / 158

Leonard Peltier

A Message to Our Young People
from Leonard Peltier

Another lockdown. There will be no Sweat. Not today. I sit alone in my cell, waiting for that door to be mercifully opened again, and my thoughts turn to you.

The editors of *Gatherings* honored me by inviting me – an Elder, they said (smile) – to write an article about reconciliation for our young people. I have thought long and hard about what I should say to you.

What can I say that will heal the physical, emotional and spiritual wounds caused by the mistreatment of our peoples by others? And what about the harm we have done to one another and to ourselves? What magic words can I say to you, our youth, that will join our hearts and souls and make us all one family – as we are supposed to be and as it was in generations past?

I decided to speak to you from my heart. There is no other way. I can only tell you what I myself have seen, the experiences of my generation.

As a young child in a boarding school, I was taught – through outright brutality – that my people had been saved from a life of pure savagery. It was my own people, I was told, who indiscriminately killed one another. There were only a handful of us left, after all, when our saviors found us (smile). We sold our mothers, sisters and daughters into slavery. We practiced a heathen religion. We had no political structure by which to govern our Nations. We were ruled by madmen who executed those who committed only minor violations of our customs. The list of our crimes, believe me, was endless. I and my fellow students became ashamed of our black hair, our brown skin, our Native features, our names, our languages, our religion, our culture and our history. We were beaten into submission. We became disconnected from Mother Earth, our people, ourselves. We tried to ease the pain with alcohol, glue, gasoline and – some of us – with hard drugs.

Others of us chose a quicker means of suicide. We became hand-

7

out Indians. Everything we had believed in and practiced as parents and grandparents down through the centuries became redundant in our hearts and minds. Many of us forgot how to love and protect our children, our people and our Nations.

Then, we thankfully heard the whispers of our Elders.

We, the Indigenous peoples of the northern hemisphere, were first called Indians by Christopher Columbus and his crew of sailors when in 1492, lost at sea, they landed on our shores. It seems this is when all our troubles began.

In only a short one hundred years, our population declined. We were as trees in an out-of-control forest fire. Our Nations became as ashes from our fire pits.

In the name of civilization, the destruction of our peoples and our ways continued into the 20th century. Our invaders forced their way of life, culture and religion on us. And, of course, they rewrote our history.

Through overheard conversations between our Nations' grandmothers and grandfathers, we came to know that there had been millions of us. Ours were advanced civilizations. Some of our peoples even built large cities – like the one near to what is now known as St. Louis, Missouri. Some of our ancestors built monuments thousands of feet high. Others carved dwellings into the mountainsides. Our knowledge of agriculture and medicine far exceeded that of the Europeans.

In some Nations, the wise clan mothers among us decided the important issues our people faced. All were accepted, especially those who were gifted. We were connected, related – to sky and earth, to all creatures, to all humankind.

When those of my generation heard these truths, a light ignited within us. Speaking from our hearts, our Elders told us, is our first duty – our first obligation to ourselves and to our peoples. So, we spoke out – against oppression, injustice, the destruction of our culture and the violation of Mother Earth. We resisted – we resist still – because we remembered the most important lesson of all. Each of us must be a survivor.

That resistance was our first step towards reconciliation – the restoration of harmony with the Great Spirit, within ourselves, among each other, and between all of humankind.

Reconciliation – The Great Healing – begins with each and every one of us.

First, honour sky and earth. Look not to man-made laws for justice but to the natural laws of the Great Mystery. By that law, there will be freedom for all of us to live in peace and harmony.

We must show respect towards others but, most of all, for ourselves. Be proud. Embrace your culture and never regret being who you are – an Indian. Love yourself.

Love your people, too. Remember who you are. Remember the old ways. Teach your children and their children. Be good to one another. And remember the Elders.

The Elders of your Nations ask for your love and understanding. We are ordinary, often flawed, and may even have done you wrong in times past. Let us show you that we have become better human beings. Let us show you that we love you. I love you. My life is yours.

Love, also, the diversity of humanity. Look upon other peoples of the Earth with respect and tolerance instead of prejudice, distrust, and hatred. How else can we live as the Creator intended, as sisters and brothers, all of one human family?

Yours is not a legacy of hopelessness and despair, but of strength and resiliency. Continue the struggle against selfishness and weakness so that our peoples may live. We can do this together – your generation and mine. Remember what Sitting Bull said, "As individual fingers we can easily be broken, but all together we make a mighty fist." Together, we will survive.

Mitakuye Oyasin,
In the Spirit of Crazy Horse,

Leonard Peltier

A limited edition series of 16' x 20' canvas reproductions of three of Leonard's paintings are being offered for sale to help raise funds so he can continue his fight for freedom. (See author Biography on page 159)

Section 1
Lessons

Mek-ee-da-ga (Putting a Blanket on Someone Sleeping)

Over the years, I've heard it said that you can't really understand a culture without also understanding the language. My 95-year-old *Kwakiutl* grandfather, Papa (Willie Hunt), is trying to teach me *Kwak'wala*. I'm desperately trying to learn.

One day Papa pointed to his bed and said, "If I'm on the bed and you put a blanket on me, we call that *mek-ee-da-ga*."

I repeated, "*Mek-ee-da-ga*."

Papa continued. "If I catch a fish and let him go, same thing. We call that *mek-ee-da-ga*."

I was confused, trying to understand the connections between these two seemingly very different concepts. In my mind, catching a fish and letting it go is very different from covering up a sleeping person who may be cold.

Later, over at the Band Office, I tell Albert Wilson, an Elder in our community, about the new word I've learned and of its two meanings. He laughs and tells me it has another meaning. "If we honour somebody in the Bighouse and we put a button blanket on him, we call that *mek-ee-da-ga*.

And miraculously it all comes together for me: putting a blanket on someone sleeping, catching a fish and letting it go, honouring someone in the Bighouse are linked concepts; they all have to do with respect, honour, care, nurturing, giving life.

A few days later I came across a picture of my mother with my baby son. I had taken the picture some twenty years ago when my eldest son was just seven months old. This was before our village's Bighouse was built. It was a cold and windy afternoon and a ceremony was taking place outdoors. My mother was holding my son, Ali, keeping him warm underneath her button blanket. I snapped what I saw as merely a cozy and colourful moment between my mother and my son.

Now I wonder what that picture might say to a *Kwak'wala* speaker such as my mother. My mother didn't learn English until she went to school at the age of nine and I know that as an adult – even after she had been speaking English for twenty years – she would sometimes confuse English words. When I was a teenager I remember her telling me that she often mixed up the English words for "feathers" and "fur." I thought this odd and told her so and she explained then that "feathers" and "fur" are both coverings of non-human creatures.

As I was taking the photo, from my non-*Kwak'wala* speaker's side of the camera lens, I saw a colourful picture: my mom and my baby son. Twenty years later and three months after my mother's death, I see a whole new picture: *Mek-ee-da-ga*. A grandson being honoured, kept warm, given life. And I've come to understand why, in order to understand a culture, we also need to understand the language.

Ha-La-Kasla.

Drew Hayden Taylor

MY ELDER IS BETTER THAN YOUR ELDER

It seems that in the simple world of Eldership (i.e. the fine art of being an Aboriginal Elder), there is apparently a hierarchy that I was not aware existed. This became apparent to me recently when I was involved in a conversation about this certain Elder that will remain nameless for obvious reasons. This one individual openly scoffed at this person being considered a wise and respected Elder, citing the fact that he once was a raging alcoholic. "He was the worst drunk in the village!" this person said with conviction.

Now it's no surprise to anyone how one's past experiences and mistakes can follow you for the rest of your life... Elders are no different. Mistakes are buoys on the river of life – they can help you either navigate the river or send you up shit creek without a paddle.

But I didn't realize those mistakes can also negate the positive achievements a person could accomplish during the remaining days of his/her existence. I was truly surprised to find out that only those who have never drank in their lives, never lied, never abused tobacco, never swore, walked counter-clockwise at a clockwise ceremony, and were never human, could be considered the only real Elders. I learn something new everyday.

I guess Priests and Nuns who hear their Calling late in life can't really become true Priests and Nuns since more than likely, sometime in their past they've taken the Lord's name in vain or had sex with a Protestant, or sampled some Devil's Food Cake. Maybe all three at once.

It's also no secret that the best drug and alcohol counsellors are usually those people who have lived the darker side of life and know of what they speak. Otherwise it would be like learning to water ski from somebody who's afraid of the water. You can read all you want, take as many workshops as you like, but unless you've wrestled with those demons yourself, there's only so much hands on experience you can bring to the job.

That's why I'm puzzled by this reaction to Elders who had a life before they became Elders. Handsome Lake, a Seneca in the late 1700s, is considered by many Iroquois to be the second great messenger, after the Peacemaker himself, sent to his people by the

Creator to teach the wisdom of the Great Peace, part of the Iroquois philosophy/beliefs. However, his visions came to him during a four day coma induced by a rather severe bout of drinking. The point being, Handsome Lake cleaned up his act and became a very well respected orator and teacher.

Gandhi, a very different type of Indian, but I'm fairly certain he can still be included in the classification of "wise Elder," was a lawyer before he became the GANDHI we're all familiar with. Now that's a hell of a bigger obstacle to overcome than alcoholism if you want to be a holy man. Buddha was a spoiled prince before he saw the light, walked his path of wisdom and developed his big belly.

Perhaps it was Nietzsche, who may or may not be considered an Elder depending on your philosophical learnings, who said it best when he wrote in a rather over used cliche "That which does not destroy us, makes us stronger." Maybe Nietzsche was an Elder because it certainly sounds like many an Elder's story I've heard. The fortitude I find in many Elders can sometimes only be forged from experience and pain.

I believe it was William Blake who coined the term, "The palace of wisdom lies on the road of excess." Wisdom comes from experience. Experience comes from trial and error. And sometimes error means waking up one morning in a place you don't know, smelling like something you don't want to know, realizing you might not have many more mornings left to wake up like this. You have to travel before you know the countryside.

Several years ago I attended an Elders conference. There were a bunch of us in a large room waiting to be instilled with knowledge by this visiting Elder, who's name I'm ashamed to say I have forgotten. Several young people took out their pens and paper, ready to learn diligently. But this method of learning was not to be. The Elder quietly asked them to put their note pads away. "Writing something down is asking permission to forget it" was what he said, and it made sense.

Not more than a few days ago, I came across a quote in a newspaper. I think the quote was from Plato, that ancient Greek philosopher dude from 2500 years ago. And it said "Writing is the instrument of forgetfulness." Sound familiar? Two wise individuals from primarily oral cultures. It seems great minds think alike.

What is an Elder? How do you define one? I don't know. Some say you can't be one until you are a grandfather. Others say it has to be conferred upon you by the community, not merely by self-identifying. I've heard some say there's an inner glow that you recognize.

But perhaps the more important question is who has the authority to say somebody isn't an Elder? Let ye who is without wisdom, cast the first doubt.

Reconciliation

We are waking up to our history
from a forced slumber
We are breathing it into our lungs
so it will be part of us again
It will make us angry at first
because we will see how much you stole from us
and for how long you watched us suffer
we will see how you see us
and how when we copied your ways
it killed our own

We will cry and cry and cry
because we can never be the same again
But we will go home to cry
and we will see ourselves in this huge mess
and we will gently whisper the circle back
and it will be old and it will be new

Then we will breathe our history back to you
you will feel how alive and strong it is
and you will feel yourself become a part of it
And it will shock you at first
because it is too big to see all at once
and you won't want to believe it
you will see how you see us
all the disaster in your ways
how much we lost

And you will cry and cry and cry
because we can never be the same again
But we will cry with you
and we will see ourselves in this huge mess
and we will gently whisper the circle back
and it will be old and it will be new

My Take on the Term 'Elder'

I think I'm sour on the term 'Elder'. Maybe it is because I have seen so much abuse not only of the term but also by the 'Elders'. The term 'Elder' has been bantered around so much for the past few years and I've found that some of the people who call themselves 'Elders' are self serving ego-maniacs. Some of the people are abusers who have gotten older and some are takers. These so-called 'Elders' take your money, give you some of the words that have been passed around from speaker to speaker and then later on show themselves in their true colours. Now not all speakers are like this. Not all old people are like this. Not all community leaders are like this. And most important of all, not all of the people fall for these so called 'Elders.'

Here in Haudenosaunee country we have some people calling themselves 'Elders'. They are older than I and in some cases, I guess, they are more knowledgeable in some areas. I have a problem with the use of the term 'Elder' because Haudenosaunee or Iroquois do not have 'Elders'. We have clan mothers, faith keepers, chiefs, and grandmothers and grandfathers, aunties and uncles. The term 'Elder', only came in during the last ten or fifteen years of the healing and recovery movement. With this healing and recovery movement, we have many people who have found jobs being 'Elders'.

Many years ago while working and living within the Ojibwa, Cree, and other nations I visited with people who were very angry with certain 'Elders'. They had been sexually and spiritually abused by these men and wanted nothing to do with them or their traditional ways. I don't believe this happens in all communities, but it does happen. This is why I'm so opposed to the self-appointed 'Elders' or community members that put others up on pedestals. We as traditional people - Ojibwa, Cree, Sault, Blood, Blackfoot, Haudenosaunee – are not meant to be put on pedestals or held higher than anyone else. We are human and there is no one person better than another.

I'm not sure what the answer is or if there is even a question about the term 'Elder'. I guess those who choose to call a person an 'Elder' may be using the term with respect and as a term of endearment. Maybe I'm just sour on the way the people choose to behave when they are given the title 'Elder'. Maybe I just wish that the 'Elders' have some self respect and respect for others so that they don't use and abuse others. The most painful story I've ever heard was of a young woman who went to an 'Elder' in the province of Manitoba and put her trust and faith in that man. He broke that trust and sexually abused her in the Sweatlodge. That woman left her traditional ways and refused to even acknowledge being Indian. I never heard what happened to her, I'm not sure she was able to even survive because she was so traumatized.

I myself experienced something of that sort by a man who was revered as an 'Elder' in the western provinces. I was at a conference here in Ontario and that man was sitting near me at a table. While he engaged me in a conversation about something another speaker had said he proceeded to place his hand on my leg. I hadn't even been introduced to him yet he felt he had the right to be that familiar with me. That is improper behavior. Now that may seem like a little thing to you but it was not to me. In our ways, a man is not to touch even a hair of your head unless you are married to him, never mind trying to touch your leg. I walked out of the conference.

There are many more stories like this. There are those who have been "guided" to do things that have ended up in tragic ways. Now you may say that the 'Elder' only guided. Maybe that is true to some extent. But when someone has been traumatized or abused in anyway they are extremely vulnerable. I don't believe that an 'Elder' is any better than a priest in a boarding school if they take advantage of the vulnerable.

'Elders' need to have the love of self, self-respect, and respect of others in the community before they step out there in that position. They need to have come to terms with their abuse and their trauma in their lives. When I say "come to terms" I do not mean they are to have shelved it, buried it, or mentally dealt with it. I mean that they need to heal the pain around it. Sometimes, the trauma or abuse doesn't come to surface until they are older. Sometimes they carry shame and guilt around an abuse that is not theirs to carry. While carrying that shame they abuse others to "get even" or because they don't even know they are doing it. Sometimes what is abusive to one is not felt as abuse to others. It depends on the trauma suffered as a child. It is when they are in a position of power over others and continue to abuse that it is repre-hensible.

Becoming an 'Elder' in the communities that have 'Elders', in the sense of wise spiritual leaders, takes a lot more than just getting older. It means having faced those painful memories and healed the emotional pain around childhood sexual, physical, emotional abuse. It means having gotten to the place of forgiveness. It means having gotten to the place where you don't take on the troubles of the world but you are willing to listen to those troubles. It means being able to guide a person to a place of goodness out of a place of anger and hatred. It means being able to guide a person through their pain in a way that will not be harmful to them or anyone else. It means having made peace with themselves and the Creator.

There is a difference between being an 'Elder' and being an older person. It is up to the person seeking that 'Elder' to know the difference. When a person is abused as a young child they often don't have the wisest judgment when it comes to picking an 'Elder' if they haven't resolved those pains from the abuse. That poor judgment may lead them to a man that others recommend from their experience but then that 'Elder' may not have healed their pain from their own abuse and will abuse.

There are some questions about what is abuse. You have people who have been abused in boarding schools at the ages of five through sixteen. They haven't had the time to grow in a healthy way with the teachings from healthy parents. These people have then raised families in unhealthy ways. They then have become older or elderly. Their children have again raised children in unhealthy ways because they haven't been taught any different. Remember you learn how to be a parent by being parented and watching how your parents raised you and your siblings. You also learn how to be married by watching the actions within your household between your mother and father. If you are raised by unhealthy parents or by priests, nuns and spinster teachers and unmarried caretakers you don't exactly have good role models. All of this is abuse to some.

The language, songs, movies, television programs, books and advertisements are selling with sex or selling sex. Jokes are prevalent that are sexual, and/or racist. Watching movies with sex and or violence at a young age is abusive to children. Their little minds and spirits don't have the capabilities to decipher right from wrong. It is abusive for them to see sexual actions of any kinds at a young age. Growing up in homes where these things are allowed, a child is being abused. Sex is for adults. Adults that have grown up emotionally mentally and spiritually to become their own person and make decisions based on their own belief systems to make healthy choices, don't allow children to watch those kinds of movies or attend those sexually explicit movies and concerts. While other adults who are not making healthy choices for themselves or their children then become older. Which older person are you going to go to for advice.

It is the responsibility of the 'Elder' to make sure that he or she is clean and sober and healthy in all four bodies - mentally, physically, emotionally and spiritually. It is the responsibility of the person seeking the 'Elder' to trust their inner selves, their gut feelings and run in the opposite direction if you get an uncomfortable feeling from the 'Elder'. If a young man is starting out on his healing path he needs to seek men that he admires that are clean and sober and walk the talk. If a young woman is starting out her journey then she needs to spend time with healthy women. There are many things that other people – 'Elders' – can tell you, but the answer ultimately comes from within you.

If you were abused by an 'Elder', then my advice is the same as I received from other traditional leaders; name names. We were intimidated as children when we were abused. We didn't know at that time that we could tell someone safe. Know that now. You can find someone safe and name names. 'Elders' in the sense of spiritual leaders have a responsibility. Our responsibility is to see that no 'Elder' or elderly person is abused. But it is also our responsibility to see that we are not abused either.

Coyote the Scientist

Time began with a big bang? That is not what I was told.

Two cousins, an eagle and a bear sat on a stump. They talked for a long time about who was who and what was what. From where they were sitting they saw *Snk'lip* (Coyote) go down by the creek. They decided to go down and investigate.

Snk'lip was watching a leaf float down the creek.

"What are you doing?" they asked.

"I am watching this leaf to predict the speed of the creek."

"Oooh." so they watched him. Soon he stopped watching the leaf and he put a branch into the middle of the creek.

"What are you doing now?"

"I am looking at the degree to which the creek pulls the branch and by the curvature of the branch will let me predict the force of the creek."

"Oh." They watched *Snk'lip* play his games. After a time *Snk'lip* let go of the branch and it floated away down the creek. *Snk'lip* walked out to the middle of the creek and placed a rock beside another.

"What are you doing now?"

"I am looking at the velocity of the water going between the two rocks."

"Oh." They continued to watch *Snk'lip*. By and by the Eagle and Bear started to get hungry.

"Catch us a fish." They asked *Snk'lip*.

Snk'lip looked at them very sad and said, "I cannot, but I can use the velocity, speed and force of the water to predict the hydraulic potential. By knowing the hydraulic potential, we can harness the power and use it to do work for us."

"But we need fish to eat."

"Maybe one day my mathematical measurements will help formulate an answer to our problems."

"But we need fish now."

"That, I can not help with."

The Eagle and the Bear starved.

   The Creator saw this problem and taught the children of the Eagle
and Bear to fish.

Oh Creator
what foresight you had
to put the animals here first
to show us the way

But your brother God
created an ambitious race
people who saw themselves above animals
they block our way

Oh Creator
do not forsake us
let Fox send us *Snk'lip* again
to replenish ourselves

To right our wrongs and restore the balance

Richard Green

Grandpa's Mystique

Grandpa had class. He had a reputation for guiding you to the answer but never butting in until you figured things out for yourself. Letting things be, perhaps, became the greatest lesson I ever learned and it came during age nine at a haying bee.

His daughters, sons, their offspring, my mother and I, plus a few neighbours came together every summer to gather the hay for the barn animals. I lived in the city, so for me the haying harvest meant a time of joy; I knew there would be camaraderie, pie and cake. For the adults it meant a time of sweat and renewed acquaintances.

As soon as the last helpers arrived, and the men went into the field, us kids formed a group and went outdoors to decide who would be 'it' for hide-and-seek. I didn't know all the kids' names but it didn't matter since they were kids. Somebody named Jimmy leaned against the house while he covered his eyes and began counting.

Everybody scattered. Some kids went into the cattails behind the house in the dried-up swamp. One shinnied up the large oak tree on the edge of the woods. When I started to follow him, he waved me away and I rushed toward the barn. I ran inside, glanced around and squinted through the cracks of the plank walls. If Jimmy came along, there were plenty of nooks and crannies to hide me.

"Ninety-five, ninety-nine, a hundred, ready or not, here I come," Jimmy shouted as he darted away from the house to search for us.

I saw him coming straight for the barn and I bolted. I went out the back and ran for the hay field using the barn as a shield. I saw a tree in the field and ran toward it. Workers drew hay from mounds and threw it on a horse driven wagon with their pitch forks. Two of them watched as I scampered up the tree quick as a cat and crouched into a wide crook in the branches.

From the barn, I heard Jimmy yelling, "I see you. I know you're in here. I'm gonna git you!"

As I snuggled deeper into the crook, a branch suddenly snapped. I fell to the field and looked at the barn to see if Jimmy was coming. I crawled behind a hay mound and somebody dumped hay on me. "He can't see you now," somebody else laughed.

As the wagon move on, I lay still as I could. I heard Jimmy's voice fading as he ran toward the cattails. Hay dust got up my nose and made me sneeze. As I sat up to brush myself off, I saw a baby rabbit on the ground in front of me.

"Hello," I said, but the rabbit lay still with his little ears pressed against his back.

I had never seen a baby cottontail before. I marveled at his big eyes, his little puff of a tail and his stillness. I wondered why he didn't run and decided that maybe he liked me. If he did, I'd take him home and he could be my pet. "You're the cutest little thing I've ever seen." I said, hoping to win his favor.

But the rabbit remained still as a stone. I decided to let him get used to me and lay down with him face to face. I didn't even move when Jimmy came running up, slapped me on the shoulder and ran off toward the house. I carefully worked my hands beneath the fluffy, little ball and held it against my belly.

When I got to the house, all the kids gathered 'round. Jimmy tried to pet the little bunny, but I pulled away just in time. If anybody's going to be the first to pet him, it should be me... I found him.

One of the girls said, "Can I have him?" Another asked, "What's his name?"

"Hippety," I announced quickly as an indication of ownership.

"Well, Delbert's 'it' this time, " said Jimmy. "Let's get going. How're you gonna play carrying a rabbit?"

"I'm not," I said. "He needs something to eat." I walked up the wobbly concrete-block steps and went into the kitchen. Big, boiling kettles covered the top of the iron stove, so I took the bunny over to a safe corner and set him down next to the wood box.

"Don't worry, Hippety." I sat next to him and leaned against the wall. "When we get home, I'm going to build you a real nice cage, probably one made out of chicken wire."

Grandpa turned a page of the newspaper. "You think he'll like living in a cage?"

"Well, chickens do," I said quickly. "You got chickens living in their coops."

"That's because they give us eggs. That rabbit going to give you eggs?"

"No, guess not." He had me thinking. I really didn't know much about rabbits. I knew when we visited Grandpa in early winter we ate rabbits for supper, but I thought those were different rabbits. Suddenly,

I felt even more protective toward Hippety. He needed saving at any cost. "I... I'll take good care of him," I stammered.

"How do you know it's a he?" Grandpa put the paper on the table and bent forward for a closer look. "What if it's a She?"

"How do you tell?" I looked hopefully at Grandpa. "Can you tell?"

"Well if it's a she, through pain, she gives life to lots of little rabbits. She makes a nest for them, feeds them, washes them, and one day one of them turns up missing. So she looks high and low and waits through the scary night when *Tawiskaron* rules and becomes broken hearted when she can't find the favorite of all her little children."

I look at Hippety and hear Grandpa push his chair out. He goes out the door and I guess he's going to the field to check haying progress. One of my aunties comes in to check the kettle of potatoes.

"Got any lettuce?" I ask. "And how about some water?"

In a flash she hands me a big, green lettuce leaf and a saucer. "You can get water from the pail," she says. "Don't be surprised if it doesn't eat nothing."

I spill some water from the dipper into the saucer and return to Hippety. I put the lettuce next to his nose and marvel at his cute little front paws. He just sits there. He doesn't even wrinkle his little nose. He's got to be hungry; he's got to eat or he'll die.

When the men come out of the field before dusk, everybody sits outside and eats. There's corn and potatoes and chicken and cake and pies and everybody partakes in this happy, festive occasion. Everybody but me.

Hippety hasn't moved all day. I don't know what's wrong with the little creature. I wish as hard as I can but he still doesn't eat or drink.

Suddenly, my aunty's standing in the doorway, "Aren't you going to eat anything? Food's getting cold."

"No, I guess I'm not very hungry."

I carefully put my hands under Hippety and lean him against my belly. I push the kitchen door open with my shoulder and slip on a loose concrete block. Hippety flips out and falls on his side in the tall grass. Instead of running, he quickly moves back into his crouch position and waits. I watch his little sides go in and out when he breathes. He's the cutest, cuddliest thing I've ever seen – even cuter than a kitten. I want to pick him up and feel his soft fur against my face.

Instead, I put my hands under him and raise him up against my belly. The sun is setting and twilight doesn't last very long. If I put him back where I found him maybe his Mum will still be searching for him.

I find the tree and the flattened hay stubs and carefully return him to his exact place. I slowly get up and look at him one last time. He's only moved once all day. I turn and run toward the house. With all that food there must be something left for me.

I don't know if Hippety's mum came for him or not. Even if she didn't at least he was back where he belonged. I do know that the next morning only dew covered the ground where I put Hippety. And when I came back from the field and looked toward the house, I saw a curtain from Grandpa's bedroom window rustle back into place.

Dawn Russell

Lumps and Bumps
(are one and the same)

Grandma K. always smelled like dog biscuits. I didn't really mind because she had a great dog and her smell was a testament to the love she felt for him.

One cold October night her dog escaped from the yard. Grandma K. in her raincoat and cane stepped out into the street to look for her four legged companion and was struck by a car. Grandma K. was eventually okay, but she needed surgery. She was going to leave for the coast on a bus, and my mom and I would look after the dog at Grandma's house for a week.

I was in Grade Seven and an expert at everything. I knew it all and I couldn't get any better. But, the night before Grandma K. left, I had to stay with her and go to school in the morning. It would have been okay if I wasn't so damned scared of her.

She was four foot nine inches tall and had been a dart playing, bowling champ, local hockey fan, foster parent, twice weekly church going Weight Watchers since before I was born. She had strength, more than I could ever comprehend.

Her husband died after a painful fight with lung cancer. They both smoked three packs a day, but Grandma K. quit when people started saying that it might be dangerous.

Whenever I had to stay with her, I always slept in Grandpa's old room. That totally freaked me out. That was the room farthest from the T.V. Grandma K. thought it was all too adult. Stuff like the news, *Love Boat* and every crime show was off limits to me. I didn't even dare peak around the corner for fear of Grandma's wrath.

Grandma K. sent me to bed at eight-thirty, an hour before my regular bedtime. I was fine with that, I was having trouble relieving myself of the taste of stewed tomatoes.

Grandma got me up in the morning to eat porridge. Yum. As I was getting dressed, I noticed a small red mark on my chest beside my left nipple. I saw an episode of *All in the Family* where Edith found a lump on her breast. In Grade Seven, a lump and a bump are one and the same. My thoughts raced to Grandpa's frail body. It was the room, the cancer room.

I asked Grandma K. if she could help me figure out what this lump was on my body. I timidly lifted the bottom of my shirt, afraid of her reaction.

"Looks like you got chicken pox," she said, then walked away. I thought she was crazy. You can't tell chicken pox by one tiny lump. She got on the phone to my school to let them know I wouldn't be in for a week or so. I tried to downgrade it to just a spider bite, but she got out the baking soda and said "You're gonna need this later".

Then she walked out the door with a suitcase. What did she know, she was going into surgery and was on pain pills.

Over the next twenty four hours, I became covered in 'lumps'.

Dawna Elaine Page (Karonhiakwas)

Juniper Berries

our people
torn from the earth
our love
torn from our hands
hey yeh ho yeh, hey yeh ho yeh
as great-grandmother's bones
disintegrate into the dark soil
so I went to the concrete city
brushed the dirt from my hands
and closed my eyes.
      my people buried beneath soil
      the soil buried beneath stone
      so must I bury my heart
      and my song
      hey yeh ho yeh, hey yeh ho yeh.
you walk above your grave
unafraid of falling
the clouds beneath your moccasins
scatter into stars
into silence   *hey ho.*
I hear your voice.
I see the moon's reflection in your wild eyes.
      come to the forest
      in the shadows
      curve the twig
      taste the leaf
      this drop of rain will quench your thirst.
our people
alive within us
our passion
alive in our bones.
my hands are bleeding
and broken from the digging
but the dark earth
beneath my nails

is enough
for One to walk on.
 hey yeh ho yeh, hey yeh ho yeh
walk with me.
let the land rise with each stride
let our tears fill the river
let the smoke rise
 the strawberry blossom
 the song begin again
  hey yeh ho yeh, hey yeh ho!

Robert Vincent Harris

Pocahontas Barbie

Tribute to my Warrior Woman Aunt/Elder
(work in progress)

Three years old, was Thirty-six years old,
she was loved by all who would take her home, buy her a drink, she is your Barbie,
to undress, twist and throw,
a dispossessed spirit, a life survivor, coping through pain too great to look at clearly,
her Grand Ole Opry was the only way she knew how to cope,

Coming down the gravel road, sounds of a muffler dragging over the prairie hills,
It's Conway Twitty, Hank Snow, and Loretta Lynn,
With Ms. Pocahontas sitting in the back seat, bruised fingers tight around Ole Jack
Daniel's neck,

They all understood her when nobody else could,
through wafting haze of blue ocean tides of smoke,
"Hey, Jimmy Reeves, pour another round for Hank,
heck, another round for all my friends."

"Waylon. Dance with me cowboy, I'll be your Indian Pocahontas Princess." "Loretta, my
coal miners daughter, sing me a song."
"I can't do that Ms. Pocahontas, it's time to go."
"Just one more dance please,
Please."
"No, I am not ready."
"Shhh... sweetie, I brought your buckskin shawl."

"Last call!"

Moist cold earth, broken teeth,
taste of rusty nails in her mouth,
frozen black hair covers her pale limbs.

Making Waves

The wind knocks me backwards as I bop up and down in the waves, all of a sudden I'm bouncing amongst the kelp patch and it slips over my body.

It feels gentle and sensuous, can't believe I ended up here. I was just trying to hide from my Ada and the chores. I knew I shouldn't have jumped into the canoe. She didn't even see me either. I just heard her calling my name. I don't know why I was trying to get away from packing water. I knew very well it was my turn today to pack Ada's water. I didn't want to leave my Indian baseball game. I was having too much fun.

Now I bop amongst the kelp because I out tricked myself again. When will I ever learn?

Hey, what's going on, all of a sudden my legs are caught up and I can't move. I wonder if I should yell for help. I'll try to get myself loose by kicking around, oh no. I'm stuck now and even my hands are caught. One big yell for all I'm worth, hopefully someone will hear me. I keep swallowing the water when I'm trying to yell.

Oh, thank God, here's a log: I've got one hand free. I'll hang on while I'm untangling myself. Oh, the water all of a sudden, it feels safe and warm. I have to keep thinking about why I'm here. I know now, I have to listen when I'm told that I have to help out my Ada.

The leafy part of the kelp slowly unravels itself from my legs. I think about Ada who never complains when she's making us something to eat. Oh thank God, the thin, stringy end of the kelp was much easier to untangle cause I could just tear it with my free hand.

Brings me back to Ada, she's been so tired lately and I could have made her day easier if I just packed her water like I was supposed to.

You know Ada always makes me feel so close in spite of my naughtiness. She's willing to remain playful and accepting so much, like our water, it can make us feel so safe and warm, if we don't approach it with haste and hurry.

Her hands so worn with age still remain soft and gentle and she touches my shoulder and looks into my eyes.

Ada sent out Dada to come out and get me on his skiff, she was the one who heard my cry for help. When I arrived she got me something to drink and she asked Dada to sing the baby song for me. I will always remember the song, for when I'm blessed with grand-children. I will sing Dada's song for them.

The Last Flood

In a land
With tricky water
Reserves
Sand bags at the ready
Waiting to sop up
Emotional messes
Of legacies
Left by Churches
Threat of floods
Permeate the air
Spins prickly electricity
Over unsuspecting vegetation

While winter snows melt in Spring
Making heavy water falls
Speed and tear
Away protective rock layers
Revealing soft brown clay
Of the original people
Pre-contact people
Pre-broken-hearted people
Before removal
Before numerous losses
Too many to mention

Dams burst open
And confuse the fish
Comfortable with steadier pace
All Hell breaks loose
With memory floods
Uncontrollable currents
Rising levels, spill onto
Unfamiliar territory
Out of it's element
Painful and pleasurable

Janet Marie Rogers

Chaos
Families can only wait
For levels to subside
Leaving once hard lands
Weepy, wanting
For heat
Evaporation
New crusts will form
New life will be born
Many generations away
From floods

Section 2
Gifts

Roxanne Lindley

The Gift

This story, like most of our Okanagan stories began many years ago.

Coyote, known for his big ego was sitting on a hill having some deep thoughts. As he looked down upon the village, he saw People who had the most undesirable qualities. Look at *Kilawna* (grizzly bear), he was very fierce and had a reputation for being very powerful; but very few could tolerate his strong musky smell. Sasquatch was someone who People honoured before harvesting and someone who could travel between the realms; however, he just couldn't get the hang of being gentle. The Rainbow Trout, a truly beautiful fish could swim sideways, forwards and backwards; however, if something like an old tree fell across the creek it often would stop the Trout from traveling.

Coyote felt pretty darn smart for being able to see these things about others in his village; too bad mirrors weren't around! Coyote was all puffed up, and really liking himself when two Chipmunks ran by.

They were so happy and excited about the stash of nuts they found, that they didn't even pay attention to Coyote. Damn them, Coyote thought, they really are worse than a couple of Magpies! As he listened to them chattering, his only thought was about how much energy they wasted. Coyote believed no one else really cared and farted in their direction, just to show them what he thought of them. Meadowlark sat on top of the pine tree and watched as the poor little Chipmunks ran away coughing and gagging. Coyote, by then, was rolling on the ground holding his sides laughing until there were tears in his eyes.

Meadowlark felt bad, and thought if she sang her song the Chipmunks would feel a little better. Coyote loved to hear a good song, and almost liked Meadowlark for a minute. But, he knows Meadowlarks only stick around for early spring and they're off like farts in the wind. They should stick around all year, Coyote thought as he looked up in the clouds; imagine how their songs would sound on a crisp wintry day.

Coyote, must have dozed off or maybe he even had a vision. Hummingbird came to him, and as she flittered about she told Coyote many important things. She told Coyote that he had pine gum in his eyes, for he chose to only see certain things. She told him that soon he would receive another teaching. She told Coyote that he had to learn to see with his ears and listen with his eyes and then she flew away.

Hummingbird was with Coyote in his vision, and now she was here with him in the village; she knew that she had things to do.

Hummingbird knew it was time to sit with the Stick People, for they were the backbone of the Okanagan. The Stick People were pretty important, and you just couldn't show up. Hummingbird knew she had to approach their Spirits first, to do that she would need to have a ceremony. She had to search for just the right plant; the one that would give her the sweet potent nectar. Hummingbird knew that she would have to gather for ten days to get the right amount for the ceremony. Finally everything was ready.

As Hummingbird went into the Sweatlodge, she knew that she held a huge responsibility on her tiny little shoulders. She knew that the Spirits would be with her as she sipped the sweet juice from her birch basket. Many Spirits entered the lodge during the purification ceremony, and Hummingbird knew immediately when Eagle Spirit came into the Sweatlodge.

Eagle Spirit always created a strong presence, and he told Hummingbird that she had to get *Kilawna*, Sasquatch, the Rainbow Trout, Chipmunk, Meadowlark, the Stick People and herself together for a special Sweat before the next new moon.

He told her of the importance of telling everyone that they were coming to share themselves; and together, under Eagle Spirit's guidance they were going to create a gift for the People.

The People would remember this gift for many years. It was very important that all those invited bring only themselves and no part of anyone else. Eagle reminded Hummingbird of the ones who had to be there, and how they had to fast for three days. That way everyone was clean, inside and on the outside as well; you didn't want to be burping or farting while the Spirits were speaking.

Hummingbird and the Spirits celebrated the night away in the Sweatlodge; she was so excited about the vision and of what was to come. Many beautiful songs were sung, and before she knew it another new day was beginning. As she opened the flap to the Sweatlodge, she saw the faint light in the eastern sky and felt such happiness that she thought her little heart was going to burst.

Her voice was raspy and her little wings were sore from drumming all night, so Hummingbird knew that she must rest. She immediately went to the tall poplar tree where her nest was, and fell asleep to the gentle rustling of the leaves.

She awoke that evening to the sounds of the drums, and realized that the People were gathered around a fire. Badger had come into the village, and had announced that he had a new wife. Badger was proud as punch as he introduced Loon, everyone admired her beautiful iridescent black necklace. Many people believed that Loons held special medicine, and many believed that it took a strong person to deal with Loon magic.

As everyone watched the two, many wondered if Badger would have the endurance to handle Loon; it wasn't long before Magpie got a betting pool going.

As she watched, Hummingbird smiled and knew this was the perfect time to talk of the beautiful things she had witnessed, and share the words of Eagle Spirit.

Hummingbird flew down to the fire, and performed a special dance in the air for the new couple. Many loved to watch her dance, she looked like a jewel as light from the fire reflected off her colorful feathers. Hummingbird had captured everyone's attention and so, she began to speak of what was to come.

Coyote sat there on the fir boughs, and yawned from boredom. Man, he thought, these two are crazy. Whoever heard of a four legged and a water bird together, he knew that it would never last. Coyote figured that they would last a few months at the most, and would let Magpie know of his bet.

Groundhog sat beside Coyote, and elbowed him; Groundhog had a very gentle soul and didn't like to have negative thoughts in his aura. Groundhog told him that he should listen to what Hummingbird was saying, and that he should be excited about the gift.

Coyote was on a roll, and as he looked down he was quick to remind the chubby little critter of how Groundhogs made the best sounding drum. Well, Groundhog let out one of his little squeals and quickly waddled away from where Coyote was sitting.

Hummingbird continued to speak, even though Coyote was being very rude; for she knew that she played a huge role in the new gift that was to be received. She knew that this was going to be a time for many tests; she knew this because everyone around the fire was being a bonehead. She knew that they often chased illusions, but she believed in her heart that the Creator would look after things.

For many days and nights Hummingbird was diligent in reminding the others of the preparation that had to be done. Everything from the purification ceremonies, the fasts, the special hunt, the offerings and the entire celebration afterwards needed to be planned.

The energy and excitement soon began to spread throughout the village; some today would say it spread like an Epidemic. Only this time it was something good.

The time had finally arrived. Soon things were going to change, no one knew in what way; they just knew something special was going to happen. The Sweatlodge had been built that morning, and everyone could smell the sweet combined aromas of red willow, fir, cedar and sage.

Kilawna, Sasquatch, the Rainbow Trout, Chipmunk, Meadowlark and the Stick People were finishing the last of their chokecherry medicine. They had come to accept the responsibility that they, along with Hummingbird would enter the Sweatlodge. Everyone knew that they were to wait until the ceremony was over and the flap opened.

Sometimes people don't listen, sometimes people have lots of things on their minds, and sometimes they just can't help it. Badger was all of that and more; before he and Loon arrived she had done her beautiful dance upon the water. Badger's heart was still aflutter; for it was the most beautiful thing he had ever seen. Badger wanted to always remember that day, so he plucked a small feather from Loon's necklace and placed it inside his medicine pouch. Just thinking of her feather in his pouch, so close to his heart, gave Badger lots of nice warm fuzzy thoughts. He wished that he could spin on top of the water, and he wished that he could have a clear distinct voice; if he could do these things he would do them for Loon.

Badger was definitely in la-la land, and he didn't even realize it as he waddled into the special Sweatlodge. All he could think of was that dance and all he could do is smile as he entered the cool dark area. Some say Badger thought it was his den; others say his head was in the clouds, but most knew Loon medicine when they seen it.

Kilawna, the Rainbow Trout, Chipmunk, Meadowlark, Hummingbird and the Stick People crawled into the Sweatlodge; Sasquatch went in last, it was his job to sit by the door. No one noticed Badger's furry warm little body, and Sasquatch closed the flap.

Everyone knew that the flap would not open between rounds and they knew they were in for a long stretch.

There were many songs, and everyone felt Eagle Spirit when he entered the Sweatlodge. Eagle Spirit instructed everyone present to join hands. Badger finally realized what was happening, and he knew that if he said anything he would be in big trouble. He knew that he would be really embarrassed if the ceremony stopped because of him. So he did the only thing that he could do, and he joined hands with Chipmunk and *Kilawna*. Hummingbird was instructed to fly above everyone's heads while Eagle Spirit sang his song; she was to fly the whole time he sang. As everyone held hands, Hummingbird flew above their heads; all she could see were beautiful bright lights. It wasn't long before the lights became beautiful rainbow coloured streaks; Eagle was bringing everyone's energies together. Badger was truly amazed by what was happening, all he could feel was an incredible feeling from the tips of his ears to his sharp claws on his little feet. Somewhere in the back of his mind, he remembered Loon and the feather he carried around his neck. Instinctively, he knew that Loon was part of this beautiful experience and he knew that they had become part of one another. This connection would last forever and ever and ever; as long as the grass continued to grow.

Finally the flap was opened, and everyone outside waited in anticipation to see what special gift was coming to the People. *Kilawna*, the Rainbow Trout, Chipmunk, Meadowlark, Hummingbird, the Stick People and Sasquatch crawled out of the Sweatlodge. When Badger waddled out, everyone gasped. Many were shocked, and Badger thought they were surprised to see him. Many had puzzled looks on their faces.

Badger heard a noise behind him, and as he looked over his shoulder he wondered what the heck came out behind him. This thing behind him was unlike anything he had ever seen. He realized that the People weren't looking at him, but at this thing that walked behind him. This thing walked on two feet, like *Kilawna* but had hair only on its head. Everyone could feel its powerful aura. What the heck was it? Hummingbird realized it was time to explain what the special gift was. Everyone was in awe, so it was easy to get everyone's attention.

Hummingbird began telling the People that the Eagle Spirit brought a gift from the Creator, and this gift would be here to remind us of the importance of being human towards one another.

This gift would be a fierce protector like *Kilawna*, and yet would be able to carry the beautiful songs of Meadowlark and Loon.

This gift would have silvery hair like Sasquatch, this was to remind the People to honour and respect the gift; for this meant knowledge and wisdom.

This gift would be able to communicate with the Water Spirits, much like the Rainbow Trout; this was very important as water is necessary for survival.

This gift would always carry the burden of the past, the present and the future; just like the Stick People. The roots would be deep within Mother Earth, and this gift would always remind the People of their responsibility in protecting all sacred beings on Mother Earth.

This gift would have the capability of Hummingbird; and would be able to travel to many different realms and would share many wonderful things with the People.

This gift would have the diligence of Badger, as well as carry the deep love that Badger felt for his true love; nothing can ever stand in the way of love.

Everyone was in seventh heaven over the idea of having such as beautiful gift bestowed upon the People. There was only one question, what was this gift to be called, what will it be known as.

Sasquatch stepped forwards and told the People that the Creator said the gift was to be known as Elder. This Elder would bring medicine and beautiful things to the People, just like the Elderberry bush does. This Elder would branch out in many directions, just like the Elderberry does and its branches would be strong enough to hold many things. This Elder would bring beautiful music through its branches, flutes would be made and the finest sounds would be created. This Elder would always gather, and teach the importance of gathering. And finally, this Elder carried the knowledge of the People and all of Coyote's qualities.

Remember that when you are in an Elder's presence.

Richard O'Halloran

Believe

When you wake up
Take your first real breath
Open your eyes and see a new day
For you are not alone
Even if there is nobody around
You are not alone
Here those voices in your head
But don't always listen to what they say
They are only there to guide you
To offer assistance
And maybe some advice
If it's good advice is completely up to you
Hear what they say
But don't always listen
Are they real?
Are you real?
What is real?
Real is what you believe
No matter what that is
Do others form what's real?
Only if they believe
To believe in something is comfort
To believe in something is true
To believe in tomorrow is hoping
To believe in what's real
Is you!

Awakenings

Rose Hips scatter about,
blessing,

Flattened dried seed pods,
dangling,

Flung to the wind as little people play,
Crickets sing the dance and sway
to the sun,

Copulating to the dance
Of the sleeping,
bushes,

Pulsing in the wind,
Contractions,
days apart,

As the midwives sit high in the trees,
The drops,
of cleansing tears.

Okanagan Translations:

Nstils	-	Think
Stm'us	-	Fish trap
Mipnumt	-	Forecaster of future
Snk'lip	-	Coyote

The Reason Why We Do and The Reason Why We Don't

Indian people... we remember. Our stories are our collective memories. The stories explain why we are and why we don't. Long before they came, with their western culture and technology.

Long before they came, with their western culture and technology, when the land was ours, we lived in a spiritual partnership with land and animals. For the animals are our brothers and sisters, they showed us the way. Animals have been here longer than we have. We respect their wisdom of the land and the resources it provides. We learned the circle of life from them. For every birth, there is death. For every death, there is birth. Something the western technology, science, economics and spirituality does not respect.

This is a story about why we don't.

Our ancestors tell us of a man. His name was *Nstils*. He was an innovative thinker. The people were unsure of him but he did seem to improve some things so they listened to him. *Nstils* could speak to the animal world. My ancestors say he could talk to the wind, the trees and the mountains. People saw him talking to a brook. The brook told him where to fish. When my people went to fish at that spot, my people ate. However, *Nstils* never helped the people give back to the fish. *Nstils* just moved forward.

Nstils was always experimenting with things. *Nstils* was always trying to build a better *Stm'us*. An old Elder named *Mipnumt* warned the people that *Nstils* might go too far. He is too ambitious and he does not think of the consequences of his actions, he said but people did not listen.

One day *Nstils* showed the men in the village a new way to fish. Traditionally my people would fish with dip nets and spears. *Nstils* showed the men, how to dam the creek with logs and rocks. He told the men a beaver told him how to do it. They built the dam higher than the water. The dam was different from the dam of the beaver. The one that the men built had a channel in the middle to let the water through.

The salmon came. The salmon had to go through the channel to get to the end of their journey. *Nstils* showed the men how to build bigger dip nets. The bigger dip nets allowed the men to catch more fish. The men of the village fished. They fished and they fished. The men fished all day and all night.

Our ancestors tell stories of the size of the pile of fish by the creek. The hill was so high. The men fished and the women prepared the fish to preserve. The women could not keep up. The fish came too fast. The women fell behind. The men kept fishing because they had not seen that the women fell behind.

The next day when the sun came up, the hot summer heat started to dry the fish. The fish were not prepared so they spoiled. The men still did not see the women could not keep up. The men kept fishing. There was never a time before when the women could not keep up. The men, when they fished with the smaller dip nets or spears; they could only catch as fast as the women could work. Nevertheless, the fish came too fast. The women could not keep up.

Mipnumt, tired from fishing all night sat on a rock by the creek. He saw the women were not keeping up. He saw the fish drying out on the banks of the creek. He jumped up and yelled, "Stop fishing! Stop fishing!"

The men had already stopped fishing. They had stopped fishing because there was no more salmon. There was not a salmon in the creek. The men searched the creek. They found no salmon. The salmon were gone. The salmon were gone forever.

The men saw the hill of dried out salmon. The men rushed to help the women. The men were too late. The salmon just dried out and rotted by the creek. The men and women just sat down and looked at the hill of dried and rotten salmon.

Snk'lip came out of the woods. *Snk'lip* sat by the creek. *Snk'lip* he looked at the hill of dried and rotten salmon. *Snk'lip* laughed, he laughed at my people. That is not the way it is supposed to be. But *Snk'lip* laughed and laughed. When *Snk'lip* was done laughing he turned that hill of dried and rotten salmon into a rock. A rock, that is still in the narrows of the creek. The rock will be there, forever. The rock reminds my people of the time they forgot about the respect for the salmon.

Sometimes in the summer, my people can hear *Snk'lip* laughing at them from the hills. His laughter reminds my people, why there are no salmon in the creek.

That *Nstils* invented many things but my people thought about his inventions in the Sweatlodge before we accepted them. We didn't need his motorized wheels, his experimental potions or his TV. We do things the ways we do things so things are there to do. Not because we can do them better for a short time.

Indian Summer

Each year my family watches the Moon's journey through the heavens, arriving at mid point on the celestial equator marks the official beginning of summer. For my family and especially for *Ten'* (mum) and me, the beginning of summer means it's berry-picking season. The white plastic ice cream pails would always be assembled and washed and carefully dried and ready to receive their bounty of berries. In the old days, baskets made from spruce and cedar roots and cedar bark would have been common. I recall that berries are also called *stoomb* – sometimes it means the meal that finishes a meal.

Since my earliest memories our family would be gathered and make ready for picking berries each summer. The prized berries were the big tame ones, the Himalayan Blackberries; they make the best tasting jam with the memory of summer locked away in jars for later pleasure, reliving the warm sun filled days during the cold winter moons. Pure cakes of dried berries were served to highborn during feasts and important celebrations. The common or lowborn people in our communities made do with mixed cakes of dried berries. We picked wild blackberries, strawberries and salmonberries. As children, we picked thimble and salmonberry shoots too. Once peeled we would dip the shoots in sugar and eat them fresh; *Ten'* would peel and steam them as the first wild vegetable of the season.

Other berries picked included soap berries, which until recently, we got only rarely from Elders or friends who shared some of their precious cache of these mouth puckering, yet delicious berries. Of all the berries, they are probably the most sought after. When whipped, sweetened with sugar and mixed with a little cold water, you get the most impossible looking Indian confection I know of, like eating whipped salmon coloured clouds. I remember the first time I ate some; they are funny tasting, almost soapy, I guess that's why they were called soap berries, sour-tasting mouth pursing experience.

I fondly recall my first time eating soap berries; it happened when we were staying over with Elders on Penelakut–Kuper Island. They were Auntie Rose and Uncle Roger Peters; back then, they were already Elders, it seemed to me when I was young; back then they seemed ancient. Now auntie, who survives her husband Roger, seems even more ancient and even wiser than those many years ago.

Well, Everett, my brother, and me were staying over the weekend with Auntie Rose and Uncle Roger and our cousin, their grand-daughter Sheila. It must have been June or early July; I remember waking on that Saturday morning to the smell of coffee brewing and eggs and bacon frying. Auntie Rose greeted us and roused us from the dreams that children dream. The house was slightly damp and the air smelled of wood smoke as well as the ocean, which was only a few steps away down the hill. The old the *:wtxw* (Longhouse) was then just down the hill.

Uncle Roger was waiting for us at the table while Everett and I washed and got dressed. They had an outhouse back then and so washing was done in the kitchen. When we'd finished we joined him at the table. Sheila was making toast. Auntie Rose went about serving breakfast, pouring coffee for uncle and juice for us.

The house had that warm, smoky, pine smell to it that you get from burning fir and hemlock wood for heat. The house was a typical standard Government Issue: level floor, thin walls without benefit of insulation, square, box situated on a plot of land. The front room was filled with furniture of all sorts. It was furnished with two old chester-fields that bravely stood the test of time with two armchairs, in need of new filling and coverings, and the ubiquitous day bed you find in many Indian households.

There were three tables, one in the kitchen area, another one with a lean to it next to the wood stove, and a smaller one with candles and bells in the corner. In the center of this table stood a statue of the Virgin; she was smiling down at a collection of burnt matches, saucers with half burnt white candles melted to their centers and various little notions around. On the wall above the stove hung a crooked crucifix and the windows were draped with blankets and sheets knotted in that typical shabby chic of Indian interior design. The dusty, bare, wood floor was salted about with various bits and pieces of human detritus. A basket in the corner spilled over with wool and knitting needles and partly finished knitted pieces of what would become an Indian knit sweater. Auntie Rose was a dedicated knitter, her sweaters were much sought after by buyers and traders everywhere.

We took our places at the table and waited while Uncle Roger said grace. He always said grace in Indian. Prayers, Indian prayers always, sound so much more real in our language than in the language of *xunitum* – the hungry people. Inside of the house it seemed as though the spirit worlds intersected with this world and that of the other newer beliefs brought here last century. There was little telling the two apart.

Auntie and Uncle also believed in the old ways just as much as the new prayers that they said. Prayer and belief was important. And like so many of our people an ease of movement between the traditions and beliefs was normal and customary, even expected. I remember reading once in a sociology text that the People of the Land easily took up the beliefs of the new people. The theory suggested that being spiritually oriented people, we found it easy to embrace other beliefs while maintaining our own community identities, traditions, customs and teachings. I like to think of this as being testament to our ability to adapt and survive no matter what the Hungry People do to us.

Auntie and Uncle were both members of the winter moons dancing traditions of the *:wtxw*. They often wore regalia that my *Ten'* had made for both of them. I remember the care and attention *Ten'* took when she made dance regalia for Rose and Roger. *Ten'* cut the designs from real black velvet and covered it in embroidered roses, sequins and tassels and ribbons. Roger's shirt was adorned with paddles and buttons. They were beautiful and I got to see Auntie Rose wear hers once as she danced her way around the fires one winter night long ago in the Longhouse.

That night that Auntie wore the regalia made by *Ten'*, sent a message to many of those assembled. Afterward, *Ten'* could hardly keep up with the orders for other shirts and other types of regalia. Dancers from everywhere came to our house looking to see if *Ten'* could make a dance shirt for them. Today, I sometimes wonder what happened to those several shirts, aprons and so forth that had been commissioned and made. Do they still make their way round the fires during the winter season, or have they been consigned to the memorial fires when their wearers became ancestors?

Thinking back to those times spent on Penelakut, I remember Auntie Rose being a good cook; the food was simple but always delicious. The seasonings were salt and pepper only; any other seasonings would have been considered unnecessary, even un-Indian.

Mostly the food back then was wild. Wild food had not become chic, but was a staple on the table and in the cupboard and in the smokehouse. There was always plenty of smoked fish and deer meat to take the place of beef, pork and chicken. It was in the early eighties that beef, pork and chicken took the place of smoked fish and deer meat on our own tables at home. Now we eat like they do: in fine restaurants when the occasional deer steak appears on the table or a "wild" salmon survives the gauntlet of pollution and contamination and zealous fishers.

On that early summer morning, Auntie served out eggs and bacon, while Sheila brought hot buttered toast to the table. The word butter is synonymous with margarine. In my early years eating "buttered" bread of any sort wasn't done, to us, it was considered gross and cruel and unusual punishment to eat slabs of congealed fat spread on bread or toast. Later I would relish the memories of coming home after school to a kitchen warmed by the smell of fresh bread, berries being jammed and fry bread stacked and dripping with "butter" waiting for us to pounce on as a prelude to supper. We would eat it with gobs of jam skimmings that *Ten'* would leave for us just for that reason.

Of course, while eating "butter" was a taboo, not eating "grease" with our fish and in our soup was unthinkable. I still enjoy good grease drizzled over my fish and rice or flavouring the soup served with frybread.

Back then *Ten'* was always jamming and canning or preserving and pickling something. It seemed we shopped for the few things we couldn't make back then. The jars of jams, jellies, pickles, preserves and fish as well as the slabs of smoked salmon, dried and smoked clams, the wrapped and frozen venison made up the bulk of our stores. The garden we planted provided us with fresh fruits and vegetables. The cattail flour and the bear fat soap which we got from back east once a year carried our family through the seasons of the moons.

Everett and me ate our fill of breakfast and then helped Uncle split and chop fire wood. Auntie came out a little while later and planted the eyes of potatoes she had saved. I remember the joy it gave her to try this little experiment. She planted them despite Uncle's misgivings and belief that they wouldn't take. Still later she disappeared for a couple of hours while Everett and Sheila and me carried on with our chores under Uncle Roger's watchful eye.

About noon Auntie reappeared carrying a small pail and a cedar stick she had cleverly carved into a paddle. She went inside and an hour later called us in to eat lunch. Lunch was fry bread, fish egg soup, one of my favourites next to black duck soup, and a bottom-up cake.

Indian kitchens always seemed to produce bottom-up cake.

Bottom-up cake was made like most other cakes except that just before it went into the oven hot sugared water was poured over it and then baked. The batter would rise while the liquid would somehow magically turn into a sauce on which the cake floated; I loved it. I haven't had bottom-up cake in years. I still remember Auntie Rose's being one of the best I'd ever eaten, especially when she would add raisins or currants to the batter.

When she was just about ready to serve the cake, she set about getting ready to make something else. She had retrieved the small pail and carved red cedar paddle from the kitchen. She was now carefully emptying the pail's contents into a squeaky-clean Pyrex glass bowl. The bowl has to be squeaky clean or it won't foam. Her movements were precise and seemed to embody the gathered wisdom of many life times.

She then went and sat down on one of the old chesterfields and slowly and then vigorously began whipping the contents of the bowl. In Indian she asked Sheila to bring some water and more sugar. Sheila stood beside her and when she was told would add either water or sugar accordingly. It was like watching an alchemist at work, her assistant making gestures and additions as Rose spoke her directions; they made sure the potion being created would be just right.

It was magic of a kind because after a few minutes the contents of the bowl started peaking from the edges as more volume was whipped in to it. To me, it was like salmon coloured cotton candy as its mass grew and grew beyond the rim of the bowl. Some more whipping and a couple of more additions from Sheila and then the wooden spatula rested.

Auntie Rose looked up at Everett and me and smiled while holding out the cedar paddle for us to taste. I tasted it first and fell in love with it from that moment onward. Everett followed next and then Uncle Roger took an even greater portion. His face beamed like a child eating chocolate or toffee and he sat in the corner looking as if he was eating one of the rarest and finest delicacies to be had on earth; it was, of course. That was how we first ate Indian ice cream and I'm transported back to that day even now whenever I eat it.

On a later visit, that summer, to Auntie and Uncle's home I made a discovery. In the garden planted beside the house and between the outhouse: masses of potato plants had flourished. Where only the eyes had been planted, with such faith and hope, great, green potato plants grew. An even later fall visit meant freshly dug potatoes accompanied our venison stew.

In our family, blackberries made up the bulk of the berries we picked. We usually picked about a hundred pounds or more of them during a season. Everett and me had a system for picking berries. We made it into a game, which would get progressively different as we went along. We'd pick one for the pot and two for the belly. Then we'd pick two for the pot and three in our bellies and so forth. At the end of the day our lips would be dyed black-purple and our fingers would look like they had been dipped in purple henna. We would pick blackberries throughout the season. *Ten'* would always pray for sun rather than rain during berry picking time.

Raspberries and other cultivated berries we usually bought from farms in Cedar or Yellow Point. Wild blackberries and wild strawberries were usually made into pies and frozen for later use in the year. Along with berries we'd pick plums and greengages and apples, crabapples too.

I remember *Khap-ah-lot*'s (Great Uncle Frank James) place had fruit trees growing all over his land and he always invited us to come and pick whenever and whatever was ready. He lived on the flats just south of Duncan. He had greengages, prune plums, golden plums and gravensteins growing on his land. He also had the best crabapples growing anywhere, which we blended with rose hips and made into a clear rose hued jelly.

Besides just having us pick, I think he really liked having the company. Great Uncle Frank would always invite us to join them for a meal when we had finished picking for the day. When picking was done and everything packed and ready to go, they'd usher us in for tea and bannock or dinner depending on the time of the day. Auntie made the best soup and fry bread as I recall. I used to love picking out the fish eyes and grossing out who ever my companions were by eating them with exaggerated delight, in front of them. We always had a *xunitum* friend or two along with us on such occasions. They were pretty easy to gross out. Nowadays, I'm lucky if I see a fish eye looking back at me in an aquarium.

Well, with our buckets and pails and canners full of fruit we would head home. There the next part of our ritual would begin. *Ten'* would set about washing and scouring bottles, gathering lids and rings, measuring amounts of sugar and taking stalk of the Certo supplies. *Ten*'*s* craft of blending the perfect quantities of fruit with pectin, sugar, and juice was just like working magic. The results were more than magical when you consider that opening a jar of jam during the dead of winter was like opening a bottle of summer sunshine.

The berries or whatever fruit had been picked would be carefully washed and culled for any bits and pieces that weren't good and then measured carefully and placed into the jam kettle. *Ten*' always used old and ancient recipes that had been handed down to her from Auntie Agnes or other Elders who shared favoured recipes with her. Those recipes always seemed to produce the best jams, jellies, pickles and preserves. They were real then; they always produced an honest flavour and made for delicious spreads and such.

Ten' would fire up the gas stove and the first batch of blackberry jam would be under way. In no time the whole house would smell sweetly of blackberries, sugar and lemon. Auntie Agnes always said the lemon zest made a good jam into a perfect jam. The counters would be lined up with hot clean jars ready and waiting to receive their black gold liquid. Back then *Ten*' used hot paraffin to seal the hot jam into the jars. And the jars were not uniform but a collection of various jars saved during the previous year's use of store bought relishes and sandwich spreads, scrubbed and sterilized ready to use again. Looking back at our practices it seems we were less paranoid about food-born illnesses, either that or our methods were just very good. Today, I'm afraid, paraffin and odd bottles and jars have given way to uniform pint jars and a ten minute water bath processing to seal the jams in.

During berry season, which seemed to never really end, the bottles of jam and preserves would gradually grow in number and variety as one berry came into its prime while another faded. Our cupboards soon filled with rows of jars glistening with black-purple, bright raspberry red, the old rose of strawberry, golden plum, limey green of the gages, clear rose of rose hip and quince or rose hip and crabapple, chartreuse of mint jelly. A host of other preserves were set by for the long winter moons that lay ahead.

Today, *Ten*' and me continue the traditions of berry picking and jamming, jellying and preserving. We continue using the same time honoured recipes and while the paraffin and odd bottles have been abandoned, the gifts of the land are still treasured and valued for their sweetness and deliciousness and wholesome goodness. More recently a few precious bushes of soap berries and their gifts have been added to our bounty preserved and saved for eating during the cold moons to come.

We stumbled on the berries quite by accident. I learned some time ago that there's no coincidence. Finding the berries was in the context of acquiring other medicine. I've also learned that teachings don't happen in isolation.

During the last several years walking my path has led me to learning about and becoming what I was chosen to be. My journey takes me between the worlds and becoming medicine is the path set before me. Understanding this and feeling that one day it'd be time to prepare, I started praying for the medicine born of eagles. To that end, I had placed a request through proper channels for eagle parts, feathers and such from the Ministry of Lands, Environment and Parks people.

At the time of my request, I had been told that my inquiry would be recorded and entered into the computer database. I was further told that it would probably be about ten years or so before my name would get to the top of the list. Well, I had figured that'd be okay, since I probably wouldn't be ready for such gifts until then.

But, I suppose the ancestors believed otherwise because within two years since placing the original request, I received a call from a staff member at the Ministry indicating that they had eagle parts available for me. He had also said that I could pick them up as soon as possible: space, freezer space wasn't a high priority with the ministry. So, *Ten'* and me made our way to the ministry offices, located North of Nanaimo across from a park, where my prized eagle parts waited collection. We stopped and parked along side a forested area. As I got out of the car, I surveyed the bushes and trees and observed a particular bush sporting tiny red berries clinging in bunches along it branches.

I'm always searching forests, beaches and other areas for medicines or just things of interest the ancestors bring to my attention. I've acquired many gifts in this way over the years.

So, puzzled and curious, I asked *Ten'* her opinion of what I was looking at; she investigated and by the tone of excitement in her voice I discerned that we'd made a fairly important discovery. She approached the bushes and carefully picked a couple of the berries, promptly popping one or two into her mouth. Well, she puckered and winced so fiercely that for just a moment as I thought to myself that perhaps witches could actually look like they do in the books I've seen over the years. When *Ten'*'s face returned to its usual human form, she smiled broadly and said rather excitedly that that was them. We'd discovered soap berries and where were the pails? For an instant I thought we'd found gold, maybe we had.

Ten' had been taught by her dad, my *silu* (grandfather) at childhood about the importance of soap berries and their uses and place in Salish custom and practice. Those lessons had taken place long before Grandpa went to be with Grandma, and now she was passing that wisdom on to me. *Ten'* had always told me that she wanted to teach me about soap berries before she went to be with her *Ten'* and dad. I recalled thinking that maybe she was telling me something else besides just what to look for and how to use the berries and root barks and other parts of the soap berry bush. Elders, I remembered, often knew or felt when it was their time and maybe *Ten'* was telling me by not telling that she was preparing for another journey. I'm glad to say that the discovery of soap berries on that day in July were just that, a teaching about soap berries and not a hidden message to prepare to cut my hair in the next couple of months.

Soap berries, aside from making a unique Indian confection, are also used to cure ulcers and some cancers. *Silu Silvey* had taught *Ten'* how to dig the roots and prepare them for making a tea with them, and to drink it to cure ulcers and cleanse the blood of cancer. I remember being told once that at the Craigflower School and Farm they used soap berries as a mouthwash and encouraged their visitors to rinse and swish before spitting out the juice. I thought to myself how very stupid the *xunitum* were at times. What with their limited vision of using Aboriginal medicines how could they not recognize the gifts they'd been given?

Since learning about what soap berries look like and the habitat that they enjoy most for growing, I intuitively began searching for more of them. Our search has taken us across much of Vancouver Island and areas that we would not ordinarily see if it were not for looking for soap berries and their promises of well-being and good health. We know that they grow along the highway on the Malahat; but climbing up the cliffs, not including crossing that ribbon of death, is most daunting and we have yet to gather sufficient courage to pick them in those areas.

On the other hand, closer to the Land of the Fierce People

(*Nanaimo*) we discovered a wealth of bushes that proved far more accessible than those requiring climbing equipment and paid up life insurance policies.

This most recent summer *Ten'* and me picked about three gallons of soap berries and harvested enough roots to make tea for a number of our ailing friends and family.

For two weeks at the beginning of June we rose early, breakfasted, donned our hats, grabbed our pails and drove to the newly found soap berry groves. During our time among the berries, I listened to *Ten'* tell stories or we spoke to the occasional passerby who happened along. I continue to add to my wealth and store of stories and family histories in this way. And *Ten'*'s style of storytelling requires that I listen carefully and make no interruptions. She has taught me how to listen to the call of the "Visitor bird" and to count its particular trills that tell how many visitors we would receive later that day, or later in the week. I've now learned to get ready with tea and bannock when I hear the "Visitor bird" call.

The incidental passerby always expressed interest in knowing what it was we were picking; and ever so reluctantly I'd share with them the nature of soap berries and their importance to us. I'm still haunted by these revelations and wonder when I'll see soap berries mass marketed and sold like any other commodity on the shelves of health food stores and specialty markets on the Island. Maybe next time I'll just pretend I speak only *hul'qumi'num'* or hide until they pass.

Each summer *Ten'* and me wander the Island in search of medicines and berries and just to be with the land as the sun warms it. With each day growing longer our journeys stretched further afield. We've picked salal berries along the way to Alert Bay, wild celery in Saanich and Parksville and Qualicum Bay. Indian Pipe can be found during late July and August. This past summer the red huckleberries were so full, just south of Ladysmith, that they bent low to the ground burdened under their own weight. And the late autumn has given us evergreen huckleberries, available in *Sooke*, until the first heavy frosts of winter.

I discovered saskatoon berry plants while visiting a garden centre and made the immediate connection between what I saw there and the bushes that grow not more than a block or so from where *Ten'* lives. We're still figuring out how we can transplant a wild goose berry back to her garden before it's buried under highway construction. We anxiously wait to know the fate of our wild celery patch that was burned out as a result of teenagers using it as partying place. I say that we'll be able to see more of it as it emerges from the land next spring; *Ten'*'s not so certain though. *Ten'* doesn't understand how they can be so disrespectful of the land and the gifts it gives us so willingly and so abundantly.

Next summer we're planning to travel to the "Elder's Gathering" in Chilliwack and along the way look for sweetgrass and sage deeper in the interior. Perhaps we'll also discover along the way family and friends we've not known before; and more summertime memories will be forged and created and reside in my thoughts waiting for transformation to ink and paper, waiting to be retold as stories.

There are many phases of the moon to come as we survey the future. Each season holds the promise of harvesting and gathering the foods that will be put by for the winter. And each will contain memories that will be put by for later retelling and sharing with my five daughters – nieces according to the *xunitum* understanding of family. They will become winter moon teachings that my *Ten'*, their *Sisilu* (grandma) has shared with me.

It's during the winter months that the efforts of berry picking season are best appreciated and the traditions and customs of a family are reaffirmed for another year. When the rewards of our efforts are eaten it's done so with thoughts of summer and with thanksgiving. When each jar of fresh jam or jelly is opened, when a bottle of golden peaches is shared for dessert, we are blessed with memories of our Indian Summer.

John Garfield Barlow

The Gift

One day, Falling Feather, a young Mi'kmaq man was walking along the shore. Clam holes were spitting, and noisy birds feasted on minnows stranded by the low tide in shallow pools. As he rounded a point on his island home, he saw a man in the distance standing upon a large rock. He followed the beach towards this man wondering who he was and why he stood upon the rock. Nearing, he noticed the man was very old and cradled something gently in his arms, a bundle that resembled a small child. As Falling Feather approached he called out to him, "What do you say old man?"

"I say the day slips away and the river will soon return," the old man answered, never turning to look at Falling Feather. He looked intently into a shallow pool that circled his rock. "I am waiting for a man."

Crossing his arms Falling Feather replied, "Which man do you wait for, perhaps I have seen him during my walk."

"I do not know, but I was told he will come." The old man raised the bundle he held in his arms, "I must keep this for him. He is on a long journey and will need these things." The old man turned and asked, "Why are you here?"

"I am walking." said Falling Feather, "That is all."

"Where do you go?" asked the old man.

"My journey has no destination," replied Falling Feather, "I am only walking."

"Perhaps your journey is the destination," said the old man absently, shaking his head at what he saw in the pool of water swelling around his rock. "Why have you come to this place?"

"The sun was warm on my face so I walked towards it, the wind, sweet and light on my back, blew this way so I followed." Falling Feather drew closer to see what the old man was looking at in the water. There was nothing in the shallow pool but the old man's reflection.

Walking around the rock Falling Feather looked up to the old man. "Do you stand upon the rock to watch for this one who is coming?"

"Already the water around this rock has risen," he replied,

pointing to the shallow pool. "Soon darkness will fall and the river will return. I am old and tired. I must stand on this rock or the river will carry me away. I must be here for he who comes, it is important that he receive what I hold. He will need these things for his journey."

Curiosity was strong in Falling Feather and he had to ask, "What do you hold there old man, may I see?"

The old man unwrapped his precious bundle and revealed his treasure; sticks, stones, shells, bones, grasses, roots and feathers. "It is important that he have these," he said, looking into Falling Feather's eyes.

"But these are just things, old man. Why do you carry no food or weapons for this man to take on his journey? Why give him things that are of no use?" Falling Feather shook his head and turned away. "You will weigh him down with nonsense."

"There is much you fail to see," the old man turned to look at Falling Feather, "these are more than just things." He held out his bundle to Falling Feather. "Take the white stone. Can you not see?"

Falling Feather took the stone, tossing it in the air and catching it. "It is a stone. Would you fill a man's pack who must journey far, with stones?"

The old man took back the stone, rolling it in his hand. "This is more than a stone I hold in my hand. Look and see." The old man held the stone up to the light.

Falling Feather eyed the stone, "A stone is just a stone, like all other stones."

"You do not see the arrow head that is in the stone? With it a man can feed, clothe, and protect himself." The old man placed the stone back in the bundle binding it securely. "You must always try to see the truth that lies within all things. Things remain things until they reveal their truth to you." The old man turned back to the rising pool of water.

"You carry symbols," replied Falling Feather, "they have no practical use."

"They are symbols of truths. Everything has a truth that lies within, and in truth there lies power." The old man tied the bundle securely and turned to face the water.

Falling Feather could see the water had risen and turned to the old man, "Come down old one, the sun slips away and the tides approach, I will help you home."

"I was told that a man will come and I must be here to pass on to him what he will need," said the old man as small waves splashed against the rock. "It is important – it is my purpose."

"The moon is strong, the tide will be high," said Falling Feather, stepping up to join the old man on the rock, "You will serve no purpose if you are swept away by the river."

"The river, like time, carries away all things." replied the old man, "I will be no different. If I am not here when he comes, he will not receive these gifts and they will be lost. I must stay no matter the cost." The old man would not be moved.

"The sun is nearly down, if this man does not come before dark, we will leave," said Falling Feather. "We can return in the morning and I will wait with you then, but you must come home with me." The old man did not move. "The water rises, I cannot leave you here alone." The old man was silent as the sun slipped away and the water rose, covering the stone. "Very well, I'll stay with you, but only to keep you from being washed away in the night," said Falling Feather. He put his arm around the old man's shoulder, "We wait together."

The rising water was cold and dark and the night was long and silent. The men took turns holding the bundle above their heads as they stood on the rock. Soon it was too deep for the old man to stand and Falling Feather had to carry him and the bundle. Both grew tired, and deep in the night the old man began to drift away. Falling Feather could not save both and when he tried to save the old man, the bundle was nearly lost.

The old man scolded Falling Feather, "I am old, it is my time young one. These gifts must be protected and passed on to he who comes, It is up to you now, if you fail all will be lost." Falling Feather tried to argue but the old man swam away. Falling Feather bowed his head as the old man disappeared.

The night was very long, it seemed that it might never end, but light returned and the river retreated. Falling Feather grieved the loss of the old man. As he studied the bundle he knew he would wait for this man who was coming so the bundle would be passed on. Falling Feather was grateful for the warm sun which dried him and he closed his eyes to soak up its warmth.

"What do you say, old man?" The questioning voice startled Falling Feather. He turned to see a young man standing on the beach.

"I am waiting for a man who is coming," replied Falling Feather.

Looking at the young man he asked, "Where do you come from?"

"I come from a place up the river," replied the young man.

"Where is it that you go?" asked Falling Feather.

"I am walking, that is all," replied the young man.

Falling Feather looked down into the shallow pool surrounding his rock and was startled by the reflection he saw there. He could only shake his head as he saw his face, the face of an old man looking back at him.

"What is it that you carry?" asked the young man.

"I am carrying what he who comes will need for his journey," replied Falling Feather, without looking at the young man. Troubled by his reflection in the water, he shook his head as he felt inside of him a truth struggling to be born. He turned to the boy, "Why have you come here?" He knew the young man's answer would prove for him the truth he felt inside.

"The wind blew me this way," the young man said as he looked at Falling Feather on the rock. "What do you hold in your bundle?"

Falling Feather looked at the young man as he felt the truth, and he held it tightly, but gently, to his chest.

The Keeper of Tradition

I am writing this to honour the memory of an Elder who made such an impact on my life that in many ways I became a completely different person. I first met Mouchem, through his granddaughter and my best friend, Linda. Linda was doing her university graduate work on Native education and Mouchem was helping her. He had asked her to take one of his "talks" back to the university. When I met Mouchem, he was eighty-two years old and a well-respected member of the community he belonged to.

Back then I was a person that couldn't feel all that much except for anger and pain. I had come from a family that had been torn apart through alcoholism, violence, abuse and social services. I had no idea of what love was. I had no idea of what acceptance was. All I knew about life was violence, rape, anger, disrespect, and hatred. I saw no value in my life. I wanted death. I wanted the ride to stop.

The first thing that I did because of Mouchem's influence was to stop the self-destructive behaviour of drinking alcohol. Linda and I were talking one day and she told me how "the old man" had spoken about poverty and how he referred to poverty in the spiritual sense, not the material sense. What Mouchem had to say about spiritual poverty and about alcohol was that for Indian people and because of our history "... there is no dignity in drinking socially or otherwise." When I heard these words, they went through me and shook my spirit and my mind in a way that made it seem like a rumble of under-standing went through my body.

When I thought about sobriety in this way, it became a political statement about who I was and who I was not. It allowed me to reflect upon my ancestors and I felt that by not consuming alcohol I was honouring them. It was a way to show respect for their lives, their traditions and the suffering they had undergone. Not drinking connected me to them and my history of who I was, on this land. I was no longer "this thing" that the colonizing forces said I was. I began to understand myself and my role as a Native woman in an occupied country.

In sobriety I also came to understand that although I continued to be materially poor I could be spiritually and emotionally rich. There were ceremonies that had been quietly passed down for centuries that I could now honourably participate in. I could live and breathe the beauty of my ancestor's ways. I could walk in their reflected beauty. Through his example and keen understanding of the world, Mouchem had been able to influence me by offering me what I had never possessed – dignity.

Mouchem was a very tall and unassuming person who didn't take up much space in a room, but you could feel his presence because he radiated warmth and happiness. Mouchem took great joy in life and many felt that joy. When I would go to the rez, he would shake my hand and smile at me in such delight that I could feel my insides start to bubble with happiness. He would say to me "If you stay here for a week, I will come and see you every day," and he would. During this time, I would feel an incredible happiness come into me. It was the first time that I had ever felt that someone was actually glad to see me, not for what I could do for them but simply because I was there. It was my first encounter with acceptance for who I was. It also began to give me the idea that perhaps our Creator, *Kize Manitoun*, hadn't made a complete mistake when I was born.

Over the few years that I knew Mouchem he continued to accept me for who I was. With Mouchem I never felt that I was too white, too dark, too fat, too skinny, too stupid, too smart, too lazy, too busy. I never had the feeling that I had to change in order to be accepted by him. But I wanted to change. I wanted to become more like him. I wanted to walk in his footsteps. And Mouchem accepted and respected this in me and helped me to heal through traditional ways.

When Mouchem left this world to go to the next, he continued to care for me. One of the gifts he gave me was comfort after his death. When Mouchem's nephew called to tell me he had gone, I felt myself shut down and then I began to weep. Remembering some of the teachings, I said out loud to Mouchem "I'm not trying to keep you here in this world Mouchem. I'm crying for me. I know you've gone to a better place. I'm crying because I'm going to miss you so much."

Seconds after I spoke out loud to Mouchem's memory, my tears stopped. I was no longer cold. I felt as if a quilt had been wrapped around me and I was no longer in pain. I began to feel the same happiness I used to feel when I was near Mouchem. Even on his journey into the next world, he had not left me. Some would say that this was a state of shock or a manifestation of my imagination, but I know that just as Mouchem had shown me that there was a better life here on earth, he showed me that there was a better life to come afterwards.

Years later I still carry Mouchem in my heart and try to show people, especially young people, the joy that he used to show me. When I was new to it I would think about Mouchem and try to imitate him. I would think, "Now what would Mouchem have said? What would he have done?" Mouchem used to go to the schools to give "good talks" to the students and the teachers and later he would tell me, "I told those teachers to just love those children, just love them". So I would attempt to show people respect and kindness so they would feel loved.

Slowly over the years, it started to become a part of me and now often when I show respect and acceptance to a young person like my niece. I also feel joy and delight in her presence. My heart no longer seems to give out the hollow sound of a rock being kicked up a gravel road. I am able to nurture her and talk to her about tradition and how it fits into our lives. I have Mouchem to thank for that. His message of love and tradition continues to affect me and others.

Although I miss him, the thought of seeing Mouchem again, when my journey to the next world begins, fills my eyes with tears of expectation as I write this. I am no longer alone, because through him, I am with All My Relations.

Marcee Mouchem*, Marcee.*

Ruby Mossflower's Magic Quilt

She lived alone at the edge of an abandoned field
ghastly with bloody carnations and translucent
yellow onions which croaked and pulsated
like a legion of eyeless frogs. She lived alone
because her husband, years before,
had decided to become a pillar of unfeeling stone.
So he walked to the rim of the blood-muddy,
croaking field and turned into a smooth black stone monolith
which was silent as a fatal bullet-hole.
To keep her busy, to keep from falling into
the sullen torpor which overshadowed this anguished land,
Ruby Mossflower took to quilting in her grey clapboard cabin,
piecing together quilts of Harlequin-checked patchwork – the
parrot-coloured blankets of a woman's dreams,
stitched with the multicolored braided strands
of an unraveled rainbow to blot out the glowering
beet-red, cast-iron sky. Ruby Mossflower lived alone.

While the blue-clawed darkness
scraped its way through the shell-thin grey shingles
of the clapboards, Ruby Mossflower had begun
a marvelous quilt, having a quilting bee with
an endless procession of Ghostly Female Quilters
which filed through her loneliness-haunted brain.
She would pin such scraps of material together,
patterned panels of cloth which all the
gallows-birds of black glass would bring to her,
squares of rags which a Wandering Ragman would
hawk like the tattered pieces of ancient maps
or like foreign newspapers from the Country of the Mad.
And so her quilt became a motley tapestry,
while the night bristled with jagged red stars and
lean green wolves circled and bayed around her cabin.

The first Ghostly Quilter who
came to her was an old Indian Woman who
was more radiant than frothy washed linen
immaculate in moonlight. Speaking with the rustle
of cat-tails swaying along a riverbank in pink twilight,
the Indian Woman sewed her part of the quilt,
adding what could be known only by someone who
could heal the sickness which spread itself across this land.
She stitched into the cloth the liquid silver of moonbeams
and the amber-gold flicker of a field of grain.
She stitched into the quilt the prayers and hopes of generations.
She stitched into the cloth the names of all her ancestors
who came before her, causing the quilt
to quiver with the milky green glow of fireflies.
She quilted her part of the quilt; and, by dawn,
the Indian woman was gone, vanishing
like an alphabet of transparent dew writ
upon a chalk-blue slate tablet in the morning sunlight.

Alone again, Ruby Mossflower gazed upon
the polychromatic sheen of the quilt, noting with quiet apprehension
the fire-winged hawk flying across a vermilion horizon.
She strummed the quilt and it twanged
like a harp of blue wood smoke thrumming
with the odors of jasmine and primrose.
"Oh my!" Ruby Mossflower exclaimed, "Whatever
has this Indian Woman done to my quilt?
What has she added to the patchwork of my design?"
Feeling faint with fear, Ruby Mossflower gazed out the window
of her little silver-grey clapboard shack,
and she was surprised to see that instead
of the bare leafless tree fruited with stinking
rotten brown memories in the backyard, there was a
yellow-leaved oak tree which she had never seen before.
"Why have I never noticed that oak tree
before? What has my magic quilt made me see?"

Ruby Mossflower worked by candlelight
upon her magic quilt, gathering the fabulous dream blanket
around her in shimmering voluminous folds and furls,
which glistened like a livid satin fresco or
neon graffiti winking across a flexible chrome wall.
While she darned and smoothed the living fabric
with her thick brown peasant-fingers, Ruby Mossflower
saw another Ghostly Quilter appear.
She was a Black woman. She wore a soiled orange-pink
kerchief bound around her hair like a turban of sassafras.
Her eyes were dark brown volcanoes of joy and rage.
When she spoke, she spoke with the soul-deep music
of blue-mahogany guitars and mockingbird-harmonicas
in a purple velvet grotto beneath a surf of whiskey . . .

And what did this Ghostly Quilter bring? What
manner of patchwork mosaic did she leave behind?
The Black woman had quilted into the rumpled tapestry
the agony of childbirth and the ecstasy of breast feeding.
She stitched into the bunched paneled cloth the
abundance of love and joy and sorrow and death.
Bright golden horned beasts streamed
from two trumpet-mouth cornucopia of amber gum!
When Miss Ruby Mossflower gazed outside of her window,
she saw not the granite bluffs which bulged
like the bald brows of stone giants,
but a Garden of Breath-pale Gazelles
grazing like a peaceful herd of pink clouds at dawn . . .
not the black night which always surrounds any child's death,
but burgeoning yellow gourds fat with the
humming sweetness of a woman's manifold, multiform life . . .

Astonished, Ruby Mossflower rubbed
her needle-&-thread-tired eyes, wondering how
it was possible for her magic quilt to re-embroider
the land as if there was power to stitch and sew
the good rich fabric of the earth. Where had
the Indian Woman and Black woman come from?

And why did they paint the cloth stain glass with
shapes and forms which she did not understand?
Three nights later, the Ghostly Quilter of the Chinese Woman
had come to add rectangles of silk to the quilt which
flared into green rice paper fans
which unfurled into carven jade birds
which blossomed into emerald ceremonial daggers
which exploded into Japanese parasols of green sparks,
Burying her face in her hands, Ruby Mossflower explained,
"No More! For you have ruined the design of my quilt!"
She said, "No more – for I fear that I will see too much!"

And many days and nights had passed and
many Ghostly Quilters had come and gone.
And with the passing of these Quilters, there were many
changes to the land or how Ruby Mossflower saw the land.
And with these changes, her grey clapboard shack
had become a place of fabulous possibilities . . .
Next Ruby Mossflower saw the Mexican Woman
enter the cabin one evening, saw the Ghostly Quilter
arrive like a Brown-Skinned Goddess of Purple-Blue Maize.
And when she left, she left behind her the quilt
which smelled strongly of chili and dill and orange cheese
and guava-juice and of the tortilla of poverty and the lime of life!
Beyond the iron-grey wood-framed window, a snow-white coyote
sang an aria which turned the stars into garlands of red peppers.

Soon, soon Ruby Mossflower's tiny
grey clapboard cabin became filled with Ghostly Quilters who
chattered and laughed and drank tea and blackberry brandy,
stitching the whole history of female friendship
which no man with leaden eye could decipher.
There was a woman from Ireland,
there was a woman from India,
there was a woman from Bolivia and Afghanistan and Iceland.
And the quilt grew and the room grew too,
and a gramophone began to play all the songs
which you can never remember but

whose scratchy creaking melody wrings your memory when you are
old. Somebody baked a batch of walnut brownies upon
which a mirthful Ruby Mossflower chipped her tooth, laughing.

While the fabulous dream blanket grew to unknown dimensions,
Ruby Mossflower – Lone Seamstress of One Thousand Lonely
Nights – gradually realized that the Ghostly Quilters were not ghosts
but real Quilters. And Ruby Mossflower also realized
that she did not live in a shell-thin grey clapboard cabin
but in a many-roomed lavender and cream-coloured house
whose green shuttered windows were open to endless summer.
Thunderstruck, Ruby Mossflower exclaimed: "How beloved
are these enchantresses of the needle and the thread
who have come to quilt my life into
one thousand panels and squares which,
like some Hieroglyphics of Witches and Sorceresses,
bespeak of a community of women never seen, never told."
And with these words, and with the brightly checked
story of the magic quilt, a bedazzled Ruby Mossflower
gazed out the window and saw not a pillar of black unfeeling stone,
but a glassy azure column of sapphire;
she saw not a field of onions and menstruating carnations
but a field of honeycomb-yellow butterflies which
bore the limpid column of frozen water away
as if it were a torn remnant from the satin-blue sky . . .

Dawna Elaine Page (Karonhiakwas)

Familiar

You came in the morning.
Shadowed sun through oak leaves
dappled your fur
but did not conceal you
Brother Wolf.
I did not run
I did not cry out
though you opened your throat
and swallowed the silence.

My father, my husband
sought you without violence
in the autumn trees
but you came to me
Brother Bear,
your dripping teeth
and steaming breath
inches from my fear,
and yet your dark silvered fur
dazzled my eyes.

I felt your spirit
touch my skin
and the scent
of your lifeblood
was warm.

I saw you leave at twilight.
Darkness stealing fire,
the last flame to go
burned in your eyes,
unblinking
Brother Wolf.
I saw no tears.

My daughter, my sister
wove you into a dream
fed your hunger
cooled your anger.
You didn't look back
Brother Bear,
when you swam into the stars.

My brothers, stay and teach me
though the woods are empty
and the lake is still.

Section 3
Knowledge

Helen-Anne Embry

The Knowledge

It's in the wind.
It's in the pride and in the hearts
of grandfathers, grandmothers.
It's in the grandchildren.

Pride and pain intertwined into our every being as we pass down
stories of our history,
Tears and blood secretly fall upon our young faces as we dance
wildly in the night,
Stories that will never more touch deaf ears, for we are now wise
enough to listen.

The wounds of mother earth,
She shakes us from her leaves, her soil,
her mountain tops and great wide plateaus,
She knows not of rage, only how to heal herself.

We still have the ancient stars to guide our way,
The knowledge of our Elders and the sun to shine to stream upon our
bodies of gold,
And the glowing moon for us to obey.

Hate can no longer be an excuse
for what we have endured,
Only great gatherings,
celebrations of feasts and friends,
But most of all, the hope for everlasting peace.

John Berry

Old Man

Old man sits alone,
With his memories,
His body aches,
His vision blurs.

Old man once young,
Once a warrior,
A Father,
A Grandfather.

Old man sits and thinks,
Of berry picking,
and young love,
He once knew,
In days now gone.

Old man sits alone,
With his memories,
Of dances,
And distances.

Old man once young,
Was a builder,
A husband,
An Uncle.

Old man sits and thinks,
Of stories,
That he knows,
From days now gone.

Old man sits alone,
And remembers,
Many things.

Who will listen?

Ojibwe Translations:

Boozhoo	-	Original man	(*Nana' boozhoo*)
Shkakmi kwe	-	Mother Earth	
K-chi mnido	-	The Creator	(*Gitchi Manitou*)
Nishnaabek	-	Aboriginal people	(The Colonized)
Zhoon yaa	-	Money	
Miigwech	-	Thank-you	

A Day in the Life of an Elder

"*Boozhoo, Wauba nungo Kwe deznekaz Wabashoshi dodem Chimnising ndoonjaba.*"

Hello my name is Morning Star. I come from Christian Island, and belong to the Martin Clan. I am going to tell the story of how many moons ago our way of life was interrupted.

I am told that this dark time came to us over fifty generations ago. Before then we lived very similar to the way we do now, except our *Shkakmi Kwe* looked very different. Our *Shkakmi Kwe* is beautiful today, but then, the waters were clear, the air was pure, and the earth seemed to go on forever.

When our new found brothers arrived from across the water it is said that they thought they had discovered a New World. Sure – we may laugh at that thought today, but our First Nations were in grave danger for a very long time. Our relatives in all four directions were affected. Life became uncivilized. It seemed as though hatred was felt for our *Shkakmi Kwe*. Destruction and despair were in store, masking her natural vigor. We tried to share ideas, but we were demanded to abide by these deceiving ways, or places very similar to the "Legend of the Residential School" would be our new home. We were to be deprived of everything that we know today.

When we connect with the *K-chi mnido* ceremoniously, it is a celebration of life. These traditions are very dear to us, and we use them everyday. They are a part of everything we do in life, wedding ceremonies, purification ceremonies, all the way to naming ceremonies. Our "give-aways" or "potlatches" are practiced to unite our people. The guests are family and friends who we care about, and the guest of honour is to give away gifts to all invited. Redistribution of wealth ensures our survival; therefore, the more that is given away, the greater the prestige. Unfortunately, our perceptions were different between races. Our traditions and ceremonies were outlawed by those demanding power. They only had one way of thinking, and because of it we had to suffer.

This culture rape tore the heart out of our people. We were just empty shells for many years. Our empty shells were misguided, and introduced to a world full of lies and betrayal. One of the main ingredients to this bribery was a form of firewater that seemed to help take all *Nishnaabek* troubles away. But this firewater was only a "cover up" disguising the problems that currently existed in our villages. Reality became worse, making it very easy for our people to be manipulated into believing our way as "wrong."

Even though our honoring of *Nana' boozoo*, used everyday in our greetings, was comparable to their belief in "Christianity," they were allowed to believe, and we were not. Basically we were forced to follow, or have no care in the world.

I am also told that the favourite obsession of the past was referred to as "money." Money was said to be a powerful trading device. We know it now as *zhoon yaa*, but these days the only use for *zhoon yaa*, is to start our fires. Other than that it is looked at the same as the rest of the leftovers from the Last World... garbage. We were competitors in a game that we were unfamiliar with. We had to figure out the rules for ourselves, but in the end it will all be worth it. As history has proven, we can make a difference on generations to come.

Thanks to the persistence of our Elders before us, we have the fortune to learn, and pass on our, once oppressed, way of life. As generations have passed, communication between races has become the most powerful tool. Now we can interweave ideas and exist unified and strong. We are working towards the land that we have only heard of, and when we have cleaned up the last of the colonial mess, we will see the true beauty of our *Shkakmi Kwe*. We are on the path towards decolonization. We started with accepting the Challenge to focus on the Restoration of our culture; developing Teamwork creates Leadership, producing Pride as the ultimate outcome. Everyone contributes; therefore, we are all equal. And that, my children, is why we need to take time to help cleanse and appreciate our *Shkakmi Kwe* everyday.

Miigwetch, Waaba nungo Kwe

Steve Russell

What Indians Want

"What do you want?"
The Question comes
with and without good will
but it comes.

"Acknowledgment of our history here!" says my Indian sister Ruth
Soucy.

"Denazification!" says my Indian brother
Ward Churchill.

These things and more,
and they will cost you dear!
More than giving the country back,
much, much more.

I think of the German civilians forced to file through the death
camps at the point of American guns,
how the civilians tried to turn away
but our GIs grimly insisted
and the German townspeople
stood there and cried, more
naked than the stacks of
naked Jewish corpses,
stripped of deniability.

Once you stand there
naked,
stripped of innocence,
bereft of "Indian depredations,"
without casinos or tax exemptions or smoke shops –
without myth or trivia,

when you stand there
naked as my hunger,

when you know the price
of taking a deer
without the deer's permission,

then we can talk.

Vera Manuel

JUSTICE

I am a product of Colonization
in this continent of North America;
A result of Cultural Oppression
by Church and Government;
A survivor of Forced Assimilation
and Genocide.
First Nations.
Indigenous.
Aboriginal
person of this land.

Yet, I do not speak the language
of my ancestors,
know little about the customs and traditions
of my people,
have never fasted up in the mountain,
have no song or dance,
no Indian name to define me,
and for most of my life
I could honestly say,
I don't know who I am.

When I look around my world,
I see my people,
in this land of riches,
confined to small spaces;
forced to fight everyday
to protect traditional territory,
living lives of poverty
similar to Third Worlds,
I feel my Rage stirring inside me.
I feel robbed,
A sense of Injustice.

When I look around my world
I see the hearts and backs of my people
breaking beneath burdens
of unresolved grief,
nightmarish memories
of childhood trauma:
Residential School;
Day School;
Foster and Adoptive homes,
generation to generation,
physical, emotional, spiritual, sexual
abuse and shame,
I feel my Rage stirring inside me.

When I allow my ears to listen
to voices of other people of this land,
who have no mercy,
no love, nor compassion
no understanding of its Unjust History,
who come for freedom,
opportunity,
adventure,
riches,
who stand on the heads of my people,
on the graves of my ancestors
and carelessly say:
"Why can't those Indian get it together?
They live off our tax money you know.
Welfare Bums!
If only they'd try to help themselves."
I feel my Rage stirring inside me,
camouflage for powerlessness and shame,
anesthesia for grief,
a sense of Injustice.
I feel unsafe in the white world,
to speak my views out loud,
to share my culture,
uneasy, mistrustful,
afraid those white people

will speak the very words I speak,
steal the ceremonies,
the sacred circle,
sacred stories, songs and dance,
then use them to continue to oppress.
Tell our stories from their white eyes and lie,
sing our songs, do our dances,
wear our names,
copy our art and sell it.
I get nervous when they write things down,
so I tell them,
you can't write it down.
I fight hard inside myself
to see the human beings that they are.

I am a product of Colonization,
the result of Cultural Oppression,
a survivor of Genocide
I carry the burden
Of all the unresolved grief
Of my ancestors
in my heart, on my shoulders, in my gut.

In this lifetime
I have committed myself
to fight for Justice.
My brother tells me,
"It is INJUSTICE that is our enemy,
not white people.
REMEMBER, we are fighting on the same side
Dr. Martin Luther King,
Ghandi, Mandela and Geronimo."

We take responsibility for our Rage,
We fight on the same side,

for JUSTICE.

Knowledge Keepers

From the north bank of their traditional territory of Musqueam, this direct descendent of the First People of this Nation surveys the band of attentive little listeners convened before him. Nodding in the affirmative (and just busting with pride), he witnessed each of us striving to be seated the tallest on our choice of favorite logs. We all hoped Great Grandpa James would notice how nicely we "under tens" were maturing. These little listeners are his son's daughter's offspring and they too were direct descendent of these First People. He knew the impending lessons would reaffirm what their receptive little hearts already knew, and would carry forward as the foundation upon which they will build their lives. Seated before him are this nation's future leaders.

Secretly, the eldest of these "under tens" (and wise beyond her tender years), was keenly aware of why we were here. You see she was put to task to corral this band of free spirits and convincing them to settle was not difficult. The allure of spending a rare opportunity with Great Grandpa James would not be missed under any circumstances.

Great Grandpa rose to his feet, each of us quickly scrambling attempting to mirror his every move. Dusting, adjusting, drawing in the warmth of the early afternoon sun deep into his (our) lungs, while scouting the aesthetic beauty of this land.

In retrospect, the venue was perfect for the epiphany moments that were about to be uttered out of the mouth of this great and gentle man I am privileged to call my Great Grandfather. I have learned never to question how he knew there was trouble-a-brewing among these fiercely independent, competitive youth. At issue was this group's choice of a leader for the first string of their field lacrosse team.

Hands now buried to the wrists, my Elder speaks of a time not so long ago where there was a similar dispute over who would be best suited to lead our community through the first of many long arduous struggles. He spoke of a time that has not changed and never shall. That is: our community is "chock-full" of present-day leaders, future leaders and leaders in their respective fields of expertise.

The combined application of these skills and experience, all contribute to strengthen of the fabric of this community. The Creator has granted each of us a set of splendid gifts as individual as we are, and each of us will be called upon at some point in our life to lead. Collectively, we must utilize these gifts and strive to identify the sources of our conflict; and through mutually respectful dialogue work toward resolution, not division.

Visibly navigating the recesses of his distant memory, he carefully chose a series of real-life stories that depicted a difficult time in our history, as a people striving to retain some semblance of culture in the face of sustained assimilation practices foisted upon us by the once "intruders," now having assumed roles as present-day governors.

The late afternoon summer breeze picks up momentum, fragrant with the distinctive whiff of freshly fallen cedars in the distance and gently depositing invisible crystals of saltiness to our lips.

We walked in silence, already practicing these newly acquired tools of dispute resolution by not fighting over which of us would be lucky enough to hold Great Grandpa's hand. Deference was afforded to the littlest of these little listeners, who were most needy of the comfort of that leathery bear-paw that held the most gentle of touch.

Specific details of the long list of overlapping stories with a cast of hundreds are a distant memory now. The lessons however, are indelibly etched in my psyche, and form an integral part of who I am and how I navigate the management of my life.

My lessons of this indescribable man have been many and my Creator has blessed me and granted me gifts of leadership, recently summoned to the challenge. Great Grandpa's son (my Mother's Father) informed me that I was "put here to help my people and that I had a responsibility to go forth and achieve."

Present-day opportunities suggest that it may be my turn to lead our people on a path toward greater relief for the many social-ills and systemic injustices our people face daily. These lessons of conflict resolution through leadership and consensus are shared responsibilities of we Aboriginal people. Only good can come from the renewed application of these tools in our every day lives, under the ever-loving guidance of these great men and women I am privileged to call my ancestors.

From the north bank of their traditional territory (on what they now call the Fraser River), this direct descendent of the First People of this land surveys with great pride the band of "little listeners" convened before her...

...this Elder quietly speaks.

O'siem

Karen Pheasant

Untitled

This story is an experience I shared with some of the Lake of The Woods Anishnaabe Grandmothers, in the early 1990's. It is about a dance our people shared with the Pow-wow dance world. It is a dance that originated in the Anishnaabe community, much like the origins of other Pow-wow dances such as the Grass Dance and the Prairie Chicken Dance. It was a dance not yet seen beyond the Northern Great Lakes region, and far Northern Ontario region. The dress, songs and dance were sustained within the Anishnaabe territory as a common and recognized tradition at different societal gatherings held by various families within the community since the late 1890's.

In the mid 1980's, several Lake of the Woods Jingle Dress dancers traveled to the Northern Plains to share the stories and intent of the Jingle dress dance. These women danced at Pow-wows, and astonished the other dancers and people at the Pow-wows. Soon, after their travels, many other women favoured the Jingle dress dance. It was some years later, when the Jingle dance style found its way to Oklahoma in the Southern United States.

In Oklahoma there was a particular family whose daughter wanted to attain the appropriate understanding of this most recent Pow-wow style of dance. This family traveled far from Oklahoma, to reach the land where the Original Roundhouse ceremonies were held.

In keeping with cultural ways and practices, this family traveled to the Lake of the Woods area with a drum and dancers and the inquisitive daughter who wanted to attain the true spirit and meaning of the Anishnaabe Jingle dress. The father provided appropriate offerings to the women and drumkeepers of these stories.

The dance floor of the Pow-wow was cleared of all dancers and the visiting Jingle dress dancers were invited to observe and listen to the stories first-hand from the dance floor perimeter. The green grass dance arbour was thick, and ready for the Grandmothers to share their stories of the dance. Once all this was initiated, the Jingle Dress Grandmothers gathered to share the story in their language, as only they could. The Grandmothers all stood in front of the Master of Ceremonies booth, with a translator beside them.

The traditional drums had their place in the centre of the dance arbour. Community and visiting Jingle dress dancers stood in earnest anticipation of the original stories. The stories were about a dream received by a Grandfather who had prayed for his Granddaughter. In this dream were songs and women wearing the Jingle Dress. This dream was given to bring healing and with the dress and songs, was a dance to acknowledge and give thanks for that which we have – our families, our lives and all that is around us.

Once the story had been told the drums started the appropriate songs, and the Grandmothers stepped forward to bring the dance for all to witness. The songs were not what you hear in contemporary times, they were the original Jingle Dress songs. A different beat, a different sense but with the spirit found common in our drum songs. After completion of their dance and the song, the Grandmothers asked all the Jingle Dress dancers present to enter the dance arbour. The women were then asked to share, through their own dance, what they had just witnessed.

Each women took her place on the dance floor, awaiting the first drum beat for that intense first dance step for the Grandmothers. The song started, each woman moved up on the dance floor within her own domain, and danced to her own awareness of the song: some with feet close the ground, some with spirited high steps, some moved closer to the inner circle, while others remained on the outskirts of the dance floor. As the song and dance progressed, the Grandmothers paused the proceedings to reiterate the intent and purpose of this dance. It was a dance done in a complete circle, with all women beside one another. Not one was to be ahead or behind, much like traditional philosophies. It was an equal partnership in sharing the gift of this dream to bring healing to all: the children, the parents, the Elders in all parts of the community.

The song was started again, and the women altered their approach on the dance floor. This time, they stood side by side, not one to pass or cross before another. All were in balance and flowed with one another, much like the water at the shore near the dance arbour. Upon completion of this portion of sharing the Jingle Dress story, the Grandmothers sent blessings to many of the women present to sustain the integrity and intent of this Jingle Dance. The Grandmothers stated that it was good to see many women and other nations adopt this dress and dance.

They also stressed that it was important to understand and acknowledge the original ways this dream and dance came to the Anishnaabe People.

This event happened almost a dozen years ago. It is only recently that this experience keeps re-appearing in my mind. Perhaps it is due to the resurgence of many tribes and their dances gaining popularity, acceptance and a contemporary fusion of them. Often times, at a cultural event, our Elders comment on the strength of our young people and their inquisitiveness to maintain our cultural ways, through language, ceremonies, or song and dance.

This resurgence, and artistic expression is a current dynamic phenomenon among our People. These experiences must be supported, as our nation works at strengthening and healing. Along with the support, one must recall and sustain the intent and integrity the Grandmothers passed to us all.

Wisdom

Elders sing the song of mystery
tell again of your life's history,
speak of youth retold and share the teachings of old,
spin your tales of wisdom
so that my children may hear them,
sing with tones so soft though your voice will never be lost,
drum with hands now worn
revealing within them wisdom born.

Brent Peacock-Cohen

Sweetness of Samson's Lion

In the words of our Elders
Lost in our intellectual past
We find an ancient concept –
People determining for themselves
Lost, though only 200 years ago
It was what we did

The lion who came filled our land
With lines on the map, with new names
Fenced our yards and said they were not ours
Denied us our language
Educated us in their customs
Which hid our traditions

The wolves that speak for us
Broke out of their silence
Through Red Power slogans
Began conversations about our concepts
Our rights and freedoms as Nations
Our ability to determine for ourselves

The eagles pointed to the *captikwlh*
Our *Sqilxw* intellectual history
Narratives of the laws that made us
In a language only the old understand
The concept lies there
It is our right and responsibility to know

In university – we see more brown faces
First People with pride in their eyes
Sadness of the past in their voices
They further a cerebral conversation
To inspire the prophecy
We are the Seventh Generation

Sqilxw hear me speak

We need a defined land base
Governance that reflects our laws
People who speak our language
Educators who teach intuition
Put your ear to the ground

And hear the cry of freedom

Section 4
Honouring

Richard O'Halloran

Thank You

Before I came you went
Into places in my head
Places you didn't have to see
You saw the real me
Blinded and unaware
You became a teacher
Offering me a new life
Free of negativity and doubts
I'm different now
My past is unfamiliar in my mind
Incomprehensible feelings
Which rented so much space
They're diluted to the point
They no longer exist
Only now I exist
I smile and now I mean it
I laugh and now I feel rested
I never knew I could
Now everyday is a journey
A beginning and not an end
I thank you for your guidance
You're my sister and my friend

For The Little Sisters

Come and gaze upon the face of Grandmother Moon.
See her rise majestic, with eternal smile,
Ancient wisdom in far seeing eyes
As we dance to time's spinning tune.

Come and dance in the light of Grandmother Moon.
Let your feet move free to the rhythm of the tide,
Your body sway to night bird's cry
As time weaves moonbeams on her loom.

Come and raise your face to Grandmother Moon.
Feel the boundless power that brings the oceans rise,
Soft, the benediction in her sigh
As she glides mystic mid time's runes.

Come and accept the gifts of Grandmother Moon.
Take the secret joy that comes with woman's time,
Strong to love with motherly eyes
As she brightens time's dim lit rooms.

Darliea Dorey

Spirituality (excerpt from *Moccasin Trail*)

Creator, endlessly embraces one's spirit, supporting me like a butterfly in flight in a soft warm breeze. When I feel despair and mental anguish, the Spirit of the Creator boosts me up in a strong embrace and lovingly, gently carries me spiritually over turmoil, as gentle and compassionately as a baby in a cradle.

Focus on the wholeness of one and the knowledge that everything is interconnected to each other. Do not take from Mother Earth without remembering to give back. Pay homage and show respect for all that has been created in the Universe.

Since Creation, evolution has pioneered many dramatic changes. Native Traditions, Medicines and Spirituality have over time proven to be the foundation of Nations of people's oneness. Their belief in the Creator and harmony with all entities has been the adhesive to many peoples' legitimate focus on humanity and the strong belief and why they are, and their purpose in life. Traditions and Spiritual belief is the umbilical cord to who I am, why I am here to serve.

In Native communities families do not raise children alone, children are the responsibility of the whole community. Children are an extension of ourselves, the continuum of our ancestors and the unceasing evolution of the Creators blessed Sacredness of Life. Children are our future and the continued passage of our people, which we must protect and educate.

Our Elders are our past, which we must respect, learn from and care for.

Aboriginal people have historically trapped and hunted this spacious untouched forest region for many generations. The land mass with the lakes, streams and dense forests have always provided enough fishing and game to sustain the livelihood of many community people for generations with fishing and hunting lodges.

The mountains to newcomers are breathtaking and their majestic size and height topped with snow caps stand high around the valleys and have a beauty which remains in the minds of many for a lifetime.

Aboriginal people have a deep respect for the land and the traditional ways of hunting, trapping and the gathering of food, necessary to nourish their lives. This knowledge has been passed down from generation to generation by our ancestors. Those who live totally off the land were connected to their land in the same way that a mother is connected to her unborn child by way of an umbilical cord. It is a bond and that deep regard for all that has been created, that you do not disrespect or pilfer just for the sake of taking to be wasteful of greedy.

This lifestyle for children was their education which moulded them for the future. By spending many years following their grandparents and parents in the bush to learn they were taught not to take anything for granted. The Elders instilled knowledge through their oral teachings, legends and their understanding for all life that the Creator has kindly provided for us to use.

There was a way of life of coexistence with one another that people respected and did not abuse. You did not waste, misuse or show a lack of gratitude for what has been provided for our healthy existence.

We often would be reminded by our Elders, to remember that when you take something created in our universe, it does not belong to you, so you must always give something back in return. We are the role models for our children, who else can they truly learn from. It is the way.

Janet Marie Rogers

Blanket Statements

She wove her warm words
Into blankets
Then wrapped me in their comfort
Protected from insecure words
Placed on cold paper
As she spoke
Words puffed themselves
Into soft pillows
Made from dream stories
Where I lay my heavy thoughts
Filled with stale remembrances

Her words released colours
Into dull corners
Her gestures decorating still air
Like wafty butterflies
With her deliverance
Hypnotizing me with positive suggestions
Relaxing tensions
With her honey laced tones

Her words are now my words
Sharing similar breath
Spoken in different times
My word weaving produces
Carpets where young ones play
Safe on dialect islands
Of silent promises
Encouraging, nurturing words
To grow on
Like food planted
In fertile fields

Bloodline

Grandmother mine
in my face
you see a cousin, a sister,
a daughter
you hear not my name
though the black river of my eyes
is sightless as your silenced ears.
We speak in the world of spirits and visions
not blood and bone
but my hands remember
who you were
who you loved
and who, in silence,
you pushed away.
One man between us
hears your voice,
dries my tears,
but the keeper of the horses, now dead
survives in the screaming ponies.
My fingers still tangled in the pelt
of the red-eyed bear,
my strength not yet in my bones,
I cower. Strike out.
The blood on my hands is
mine Grandmother
hear me,
see in my eyes the stone
worn smooth by the river.

Dawna Elaine Page (Karonhiakwas)

For All My Relations
(Katie Tarbell Herne, 12/17/1899—7/31/2000)

one
hundred years ago
we buried the stone
beneath the birch tree

one
hundred years ago
our grandmother was born
a child of change
            turning centuries
            tangled cultures
weaving old and new
into her cradle board
many knots were tied

one
hundred hours ago
our grandmother closed her eyes
one
last breath
held
one hundred years of history
a basket filled with feathers —
carrying water, driving horses,
the ringing of iron and laughter
calling us home
to play cards
tell stories
and listen

Listen.

her words
will be buried with her
in the darkness

trees and rivers
become shadows
in the silence

but the drum beats
in one heart
the water washes the stone
and the birch leaves fall
as one
hundred tears

Dawna Elaine Page (Karonhiakwas)

March Moon

Grandmother Moon,
smile upon my daughter
and me
as we splash like otter children
in a bath of foam.

Grandmother Moon,
beam blessings upon my daughter
and me
as we gaze on your reflection
in a river of blood.

Grandmother Moon,
shower peace upon my daughter
and me.
Your ancient face shines down
through the silver rain.

May your celestial countenance
always remind my daughter
and me
of our Mother
Earth's womb
in whose waters we still swim.

You are the Clan Mother
of our heavenly ancestry
the spirit guide
of our sail in the cosmic sea

Even when your waters
no longer wash our shores,
bleach our bones like shells
and remember
my daughter and me,
Grandmother Moon.

Silent Drum

Time whispers by. There is no comparison to its stealthy drip, but it feels so much like a drumbeat in slow motion, a memory of sweetgrass in July. I am young and still tiptoe around the earth, pondering questions, wondering at new springs, yet each year feels shorter and I feel lost in the movement of things so much that at times my heart beats silently still. This awareness has opened the eyes of the owl in me, and ripped out the child. I sit here in the vastness of things and feel time push me forward with wind-nudges and earthy brown silences.

When my son was born, he had the eyes of my father in death. The definitive depth of knowledge that pierced into my mind-sense and pulsed into my temples. The beginning and ending of knowledge, the entire swim of the senses colliding into a first and a last. Eyes that stalled my heart with the wisdom of fullness. I tasted the whole for some sharp second with each of their stares until slowly I forgot the taste of their pungent intensities and fell back into the walk of my learning. What is it in those final and first seconds that expose themselves to us observers? My mind is a fancy dance of questions, ones which I forget, ones which I fear.

My father was a storyteller. His eyes were songs which danced us to the moon at night. Over the years we'd heard thousands of his adventures, his memories. We could trace the scars on his skin and know of his battles. My sisters and I would gather at his feet and know that he had seen the world, lived it, tasted the streets with the relish of a bear in springtime. Our daddy was wise. But that was all before he got sick. One day the stories stopped. He was silenced by tubes, machines, morphine. His stories lay buried under his wealth of blankets that lay over him like the field of grass behind Grandma's house, where she said the coyotes roamed at night. He was a fly in a web of tubes, a vault of knowledge slammed shut before we had gotten our fill.

At nights I would peek into his room to look at him. I was too scared to see in the day, when birds would brag their freedom to him from his view out of the big living room window. I would scurry through the house, eyes downcast muttering to myself, knowing that if I asked him a question he would answer in his unfamiliar robotic voice, the tube vibrating in his throat, as clear as a thousand angry bees. Soon, he almost stopped talking altogether. No one to hear, no one to listen. It was his silence that provoked my discomfort. His voice to me was the colour of his life, and nights were the only time I could manage such silences, with the howl of the wind to comfort me. His slow death seemed appropriate at midnight, when life was in hiding. I would trace his shrunken body lined under the sweat soaked sheets, remembering his tales of the residential school, the army, his years on the streets. I would wait until my eyes adjusted to the dark and find his tattoos on his arms, the ink turned greenish from age, and think that once his arm-skin was a clear brown when he was a boy. The progression of age, of time's rapid movement was too incomprehensible then, so I ran, ran and let my daddy die a silent man, his eyes watching me under the dark, dark midnight moon.

Death happened like a passing train. We knew it was time. We waited, gathered, sensing its arrival, circling his bed, waiting for the headlights to appear. We heard its sound first. An increase in breath, chug-chug-chug-chug, a buzz in our ears, a pounding of our own heartbeats increasing with his breaths; the sound of darkness tugging at our senses. Daddy's eyes opened. They saw everything at once, held such knowledge of living that my mind swam. He held the elements in his eyes, became hunger and thirst, animal and plant, heavy and lightness. My senses edged toward pain, my throat opened and closed along with his. The train passed by, whipping forward like a perfectly slung arrow, making the earth tremble, our legs tremble. Trembling. And then the caboose. Always wave goodbye to the caboose. My arm raised goodbye. CHOO-CHOO!! I slowly watched his mouth close into a silence more pure, more tranquil than his last voiceless year.

Standing by his grave, I am furious at my own voicelessness his last years. There were more. Stories. Untold stories. I want to inhale them out of his body as I stand over the thick, earthy mound, and let them sink into me, teaching me his life-walk, making his knowledge more complete, more a part of me. There is so much that he had taken with him. I didn't realize then how much he left behind, how much he'd still give over the years.

My son was born howling, skin rage-red, eyes wide open searching for me. When our eyes connected, I felt my daddy again, laughing somewhere, the past twirling into the now like smoke rising from a peacepipe. I was in the middle of life for the first time, knowing the fullness, the connectedness, the circular path of everything. I was underwater, sky-bound at once, the Salmon and the Eagle sharing one being, and I knew where daddy went in his silences at last. I found him once again. His knowledge has found me outside of death, opened wide, pouring into me to offer to my son.

I can relax now, hear the winds speak to me during my own silences. My worry has been absorbed into the ground, sucked down hungrily. I watch my small son lay on his blanket, the grass licking his heels, and understand that knowledge is ebbing into him each second with each new leaf he sees in the tree above. I sit between all directions, just him and I, dreaming of the now. I am quietness, and the world around me pulses, holds me in its drumbeat.

Lesley Belleau

Indian Eyes

Draped here: somewhere between your
constant prodding
and clay-tinged existence
I begin a ride of earthed-edged journey,
tiptoeing around the urgency
of your rabbit kicks and my own startled heart.

My father died
an Indian with volumes of silenced tongues
in his palms.
He wanted a boy to shoot a baseball to in our dirt-drenched
reservation yard.
Us girls instead flattered him with brownies from our
Easy Bake Ovens
Our ball gloves lint-filled under Barbie dresses.

Now you are here baby boy
Inside of me,
and your movements are like my father's fast earth walk.
No whispers here
but drumbeats that fancy-dance under
my line of even rib.

I know you see him Daddy. He will throw a ball clear over
the power lines. Why couldn't you wait for him?

Draped here: in this place of winter silence
That I colour-fill with hints of crimson living
I go back to little feet that play hide and seek
with my fingers
somewhere in her tight-skinned belly,
and dream that my father's quick
Indian eyes are
watching
our earth history play itself out.

Going Home

"Wow, that's cool – you don't see this in the city," Warren thought to himself as he gazed out of the cabin window. Outside, visibility was about two hundred yards and getting worse as the wind increased and the sun set. Looking at the pine trees, he imagined them groaning as they bent from the gusts of wind; they would moan in unison, their branches reaching out for something. "What are they reaching for?" he thought, as he became lost in his imagination. "Maybe there's something out there we don't see... maybe spirits, maybe those bad pointy-nose people Moshum calls "*PAKAKOOS*," he mused, remembering the legends. Those people of the forest that were always there and if you didn't watch it, they would lead you deep into the forest – lost forever. They were white as the snow with long noses that stuck straight out from their faces, like branches of a tree, and they didn't talk. Their legs, arms, and hands were gnarled, knotted and so skinny, like the skin of peeling bark. They would motion with these hands, smiling all the time to follow them. "This way," they would seem to say..." Come, over here, no-no, this way, follow me."

BANG, BANG! Warren almost fell to his knees; someone was knocking at the door. He stood there paralyzed, his heart loud in his ears, so loud, in fact, that he began to think that it was his heart he had heard and not the door.

BANG, BANG! Again, he jumped, no imagination this time. He moved further from the door and over to the window near the table where Moshum and Kokum were sitting. They smiled at each other, no surprise on their faces as his stare turned to the door.

"*PEETAKWAY*! COME IN!" Moshum hollered as Warren jumped for the third time.

"Don't do that, Mosh!" Warren exclaimed.

"What?" Moshum asked with a smile getting bigger.

"Holler like that!"

"Oh, sorry.... what you jumping around here for? Better go answer the door."

At that moment the door opened with a howl, as a sheet of snow came dancing in. A figure emerged from the darkness outside into the orange glow of the interior. Squinting his eyes, Warren realized it was

Mrs. J., the old lady that lived by herself about two miles down the road.

"What the heck is she doing here in this weather?" he thought, glancing from her to the window repeatedly.

Moshum and Kokum both got up, shaking her hand warmly, then motioned for her to sit down. They spoke in Cree as they sat around the table drinking tea, then playing cards late in to the night. Warren could make out the conversation in bits and pieces from the Cree he knew, and as far as he could tell, they weren't really talking about anything in particular – just small talk. But, to him, this was unusual, a mystery that this elderly lady would come at night in this weather, then just sit around and talk. He liked Mrs. J., but she didn't speak to children much. Whenever she looked at Warren, it was with a warm smile, more in her eyes than in her mouth. Listening to the wind outside and the hushed voices around the kerosene lamp, he soon drifted off to sleep.

He awoke to the creaking of the stove's oven door, glancing sideways, he saw Kokum taking out some bannock, using tea towels as oven mitts. In ten seconds Warren was dressed and at the table eating steaming hot bannock smothered with margarine and homemade strawberry jam. Having satisfied his hunger, his thoughts turned to the events of last night. Noticing the calm outside, he realized Mrs. J. was gone.

"Kokum, where's Mrs. J.?"

"Oh, she's gone. She left around two in the morning. Hooked up the horses and went home."

"Really? Why did she come in the first place? In this weather?" Warren asked in complete amazement.

"She does that whenever a storm is brewing. It brings back some old memories, and I guess she likes somebody to talk to at those times."

"Why? What memories?"

Kokum sat down then, slowly. With a tea towel in her hands, flour on her face, she began in a whisper. "Well... not long ago, there used to be Missionary schools – do you know about them, Warren?"

"Yeah, a bit. I heard that when kids reached a certain age, they were forced to go to school far away from their families and sometimes not come back till they were sixteen or eighteen."

"Right! This was compulsory. Families had no say and many would cry when this time came. Some would move or hide their young when the Indian Agents or priests would come around, counting how many kids they had, and how old they were. It was a sad time. Mrs. J. never did go to school, you know. She was about six years when they came around to pick up kids for the Mission School. They took her older brother, Matthew, who she adored. He was about eight years old at the time, and she was too young. Ages for school were a little different then. Her mom and dad were heartbroken and she cried many nights for her older brother. She says she can still see so clearly the memory of her brother being cramped into the back of a truck along with twenty other kids, and as they drove off, the look on his face, scared and sad. Those sad, sad eyes... Anyway, things kind of returned to normal, although they missed him terribly at Christmas time. Christmas and Easter during those years were different too, mainly celebrated by the white people, but there were still special – a time for families to gather."

"I think it was close to Easter, when word came through the Indian Agent that Matthew was ill, and for his dad to come and get him. Apparently, all this time, Matthew had been homesick –very homesick, and nobody thought it was serious. So, his dad hurried, got some blankets, some food, and Matthew's favourite horse, a white horse. To them, this was a joyous time, they would all be together soon. Mrs. J. was so happy, she loved her family. With her brother back, she knew her mom and dad would be like they were before. Her Dad left right away, traveling for two days on horseback, for it was a long ways away. Mrs. J. and her mother figured it would be four or five days when they would be home. So, to keep themselves busy, they planned on cooking, baking – all things Matthew loved. Those five days turned to six, then eight days. By this time, they were worried. Something must have happened, maybe Dad had injured himself, or gotten sick. With help from the local priest and other families, they began a search. After two days, they found them. In the middle of a prairie, they saw a white horse standing by himself. Coming closer, they could make out a mound of snow beside the horse. Clearing off the snow, they could see blankets and under these, Matthew and his dad, frozen. The boy was wrapped up in blankets and around him, his father had him in his arms, as if to keep him warm. What happened before this is really sad. After reaching the Mission, the father learned his son, Matthew had passed away – probably from a broken heart, there was no other explanation. Gathering his son's belongings, he immediately set out for home – against the advice of the school. They were concerned because winds were picking up with the temperature getting to fifteen below. In his grief, he heard little and was not aware of the weather. A white-out must have happened – you know, Warren, when everything turns white and you become lost. He must have laid down with his son whom he had placed on a makeshift travois wrapped in blankets. With the cold winds beating at him and playing tricks with his mind, they figured he must have taken off his own blanket and wrapped it around Matthew to try and save his poor son's life.

Mrs. J. never forgot and never stopped grieving. Her mother was never the same, and died a couple of years later, leaving Mrs. J. alone. She was brought up by her uncle, who was very loving, but that time still haunts her. She never did go to school after that. She got married young and was happy with her own kids and after awhile, grandchildren, too. Her husband, Mr. J., passed away when he was sixty-five – they'd been married for forty-five years and she's around eighty now.

Warren contemplated, he sat quietly now, facing the window. In his mind, he visualized this tragic scene; his eyes open, but blind to this world, he saw the story unfold and replay before him. Entranced, he thought... this is one story he would not forget.

Homelands

Where the fires,
Of Creator still shine,
In the night.

Past the nests,
Of metal city lights,
Reflected in the sky.

Where the hills rise,
Towards the hawk's flight,
Above.

Past the scars,
Of Power lines,
Upon mothers skin.

Where the roads end,
And deer's path leads you,
Onward.

Past the stench,
Of modern life,
Find Eagle in flight.

This is Indian Country,
Hear the beating,
Of your heart.

Remember the land,
Breathe deep,
And go on.

John Berry

Sundown

Standing with the old men,
Before the glory,
Of the red and purple sunset,
Giving thanks.

With thanks,
For another day,
Of breath and life,
With my relations.

Speaking without talking,
Before Creator,
With thanks,
For what is given.

Days end will come,
To us all,
May we go on,
With thanks.

Standing straight and clean,
At sundown,
Of another day,
Give thanks.

John Berry

Reflections on Water

Sitting by water I look,
    and see it move without effort,
        around, over, under, through,
            the bones of the earth.

Clear and pure it flows like the people's spirit,
    like our stories told,
        by the old people,
            without seeming effort.

The stones resist patiently, sometimes angrily,
    like other peoples who deal with us,
        many colored and shaped and hardened,
            smooth, rough, round, angular, all kinds.

The water covers them all,
    it covers and moves the stones,
        without effort or judgement,
            enduring it moves mountains.

Finally, the water will win,
    cleansing and purifying,
        it's victory is final,
            the stones disappear.

Moving without effort,
    our spirit and stories will endure,
        our victory in time, will be,
            like water.

Wings of the Morning

"... In thy book were written, every one of them, the days that were formed for me, when as yet there were none of them..."

Psalm 139

The early morning haze in the eastern sky mixed with smoke from a lingering forest fire and set the heavens brilliantly aglow.

I was riding in a taxi on my way to the Goose Bay airport to catch the thirty-five minute flight to Rigolet on Labrador's north coast. Over the car radio, Great Big Sea blared out *"Ordinary Day."* The taxi driver, taking on the role of weatherman, told me that we would be in for another hot one.

I was relieved to be leaving Goose Bay.

Rigolet, the Inuit community where I was born, was always special to me, especially in July. There, I could catch some of the smells from the ocean and feel the easterly wind. The cold wind that often comes in from the North Atlantic in the evenings following hot summer days is what we called the "in wind."

I paid the taxi driver and carried my bags into the terminal building. After I finished checking at the ticket counter, I turned to walk into the coffee shop.

It was then that I saw her.

I blinked and as I did, some thirty-five years of my life were suddenly erased and I stood transfixed before events of my childhood. My heart raced as our eyes locked. It seemed like a giant wave had engulfed me and transported me to another place and time. I believe I felt the workings of a higher power.

This was no accidental meeting, and it would not be any ordinary day like the song had been saying on the radio.

Her eyes were as soft as ever and her smile just as gentle. Maybe even more so now that she had matured into the beautiful lady that she'd become.

As we greeted each other, our conversation naturally drifted back to the time when we first met.

Her presence was magic. In the booth together over coffee, I may as well have climbed into a time machine. Memories of long ago crowded our thoughts and our conversation. Memories of things that I thought I had forgotten… until now.

In those moments, I went back to the Labrador I knew as a child… the Labrador of the 1960s.

I was thirteen in September 1965.

The changing season at that time of year makes the chill from the fall winds seem menacing. The people of Rigolet would soon awaken to an accumulation of snow on the surrounding hilltops.

It is a time for counting down days to when we can expect the single-engine beaver to pay a visit. Julia Alpha Tango was the small, red bush plane used mainly for mercy flights for the hospital. The medical missionaries who ran the hospital and the school dormitory in North West River, were known as the International Grenfell Association. The "mission."

This September day though, the plane's arrival would not mean a visit from the nurse or the doctor. Neither will it come to take a patient away to hospital. This time its mission is to take me and several other children away from our families in Rigolet.

The school year is about to begin.

September became a time of parting, a time of fear, a time of feeling that dull, nauseous pain in the pit of my stomach. It was also a time when my mother would weep in public as she'd hug and say good-bye to us.

As the floatplane touches down on the waters of the bay, a feeling of sadness and gloom settles over those awaiting its arrival. Taxiing to the wharf, the propeller slows and comes to a stop.

There is no time left. I am placed aboard the plane and readied for the flight to North West River, I crane my neck so as to look back through the window and hope that they will see my wave. I try to put on a brave face as I catch a last glimpse of Mom and Dad. Her hands are up to her face. My Father is holding her arm and walking beside her… my little brother tags along behind.

Feeling as though I am about to enter an unknown world, I settle back into my seat, not knowing how to prepare for the rest of my life. A surge of pain starting as a choking feeling in my throat runs to my stomach and all the way to my bowels, when I am struck by the reality that it will be a full ten months, before I will see my family again. I am already homesick. I think of things that I should have said before I left but didn't. I think of hurtful, childish words that I would say now and then, to my mom and dad, and to my grandmother, and to my eight year old brother. I wished that I could have just a few more moments back there with them to tell them that I never meant any of those things... that I am sorry... that I love you.

Education came at a steep price in Labrador in the 1960s.

As the plane takes off its engine revs so loudly that it can be heard for miles. It lifts from the water and climbs in the air toward Sand Banks on the other side of the bay and turns west toward North West River. The echo of its engine off the hills seems to announce our departure. It is a lonely, hollow sound to those left behind in Rigolet. In an hour or so, I will begin a new life among strangers.

When I met her, she had already spent a year at the dorm and was familiar with the place and some of the people. She must have thought I was a little timid the first time we spoke.

I had trouble fitting in. The place was foreign to me. It was the first time I had seen modern things like a motor vehicle, telephones and flush toilets.

Some people liked to make fun of the way I spoke with a noticeable "down-the-bay" accent. I was ashamed and didn't feel good enough.

Now when I think about life in the dorm with the fifty or so other children, under the strict guidance of house parents, I think about loneliness. I think about unappetizing food. I think about fear of the unknown and a sense of survival of the fittest, with no one to talk to who would listen or understand. Except you.

I think about how we became distanced as brothers and sisters. It seemed to be expected that the price of fitting in, was not to consider a sibling as a brother or sister, but as just another dorm kid. Recalling this brought a painful emotion as I thought of some of the incidents that led me to that conclusion.

Back then, you listened to me and did not seem to mind my timidness. Now as we sat waiting for our flights, her question to me about abuse came as a surprise.

I thought for a long moment. Though I may not have experienced physical or sexual abuse, I told her, the system itself was one that caused the break up of generations of families in Labrador. For many years, I have debated with myself, whether or not this could have been abuse... because there are plenty of hidden scars, I said... and they are just as real as those you can see. Behind each is a story waiting to be told.

She understood.

"Have you forgiven?" she asked. "I believe I have."

"Tell me more," I said.

She told me many things about her life after the dorm… a rocky road over which she had gone astray but found her way back. She ended by speaking words from the *Old Testament* that "..if I take the wings of the morning, and dwell in the uttermost parts of the sea, even there thy hand will lead me…"

"*Psalm 139*," she said. "I read it often, and each time I do I find peace and wisdom. If you are looking for answers, maybe you will find something there too."

I thanked her for listening and trying to understand me in the mid-60s… and for this journey again today.

"I love you Billy", she said through eyes of mist.

We embraced for a long moment before heading to security. I felt the tide rush out again and I believe I savoured the taste of freedom.

We flew north and to the east, toward the freshness of a new day.

Half an hour later, the twin otter landed at the airstrip in Rigolet.

I found that I could not wait to get to my father's house and open the *King James version* to *Psalm 139*.

The words that unfolded in front of me were stunning. I might have read them somewhere, sometime, before, but if I did, they were just words on a page. Now, it was as though I could hear her voice reading to me in 1965. I swear that she could have written that passage. She has lived her life by these words. Never hating. Ever loving. Everlasting.

I will consider my journey a success if I can live the rest of my life being half the person that you are.

I will follow you.

Dear Beloved Child

Written for you, to let you know how wonderful it is to have you on this earth with us. I understand that life has put difficult things in your path. I just want to say, not to despair and that healing does come when we are ready to receive it.

I would like to share my story as a survivor of abuse to encourage you to go on with your life. I know it's very hard to overcome our hurts and to forgive our aggressor/s. It takes time and a lot of hard work to face them. When I was first asked to write this letter, I had a very hard time to find the right words to say. You see, I do not wish to burden you with sadness but to shed some light on our common darkness.

It took a long time for me to face my abuse and I wondered around this world looking for love in the wrong places. I thought I could find one person to love, care and listen to me and tell me that everything will be alright. I went through my teenage years in such turmoil and I confess that I too was at risk to commit suicide. I wanted to crawl out of own skin and leave this loneliness and pain behind.

One day, I was given an awakening that affirmed my abuse. And I remembered where, when and who it happened with. I remember that day very clearly and how I felt. I shook very violently, and I cried with all the energy I could muster. I wept in anger, in shame, insanely for the innocence I have lost. I felt so betrayed and robbed of my spirit, my physical, my mental and emotional being. I could not sleep for a whole week and fear flooded my world. I finally realized that I could no longer keep this terrible secret inside me. I needed to tell whoever would listen, and called for help to release my madness. The hurt and pain I felt that day was so real and clear in my mind. Slowly, in the next few years that followed I felt like I was in Hell. I made some major decisions to get help and begin my healing journey. I began to put tobacco at a special tree where I would leave my fears and pain. I searched for elders to calm my broken spirit and restore my health. I thank the Creator for all the people that crossed my path to help me as I began my healing. I didn't think I would see the light of day because even the brightest day looked so gloomy. But as each day went by I got stronger and able to lift myself up again. It was a bright new day for me when I came through the first stage of my shedding my pain. I had carried so much on my back that I was bent over like a hunchback.

Now I look back and laugh about it with my friends who care, and with my family too. I am able to take a second look at all the turmoil and learned to forgive my aggressor as I began to understand where all the abuse was coming from. The real joy in healing is to be able to say to the aggressor, I forgive you and I love you. Though, I have my ups and downs, I am able to get up in the morning and say to the reflection in the mirror, You are special and You will be fine.

I am sure the Creator will bring abundance to your needs as you begin a healing journey. So, today I would like to extend this unconditional love to you, Beloved Child. You are special and the Creator has put you on this earth for a purpose.

May the Great Mystery, Great Spirit guide and protect you on your journey.

Section 5
International
and
Words from our Youth

International

Reconciliation: Elders as Knowledge Keepers

Today I am a strong-minded independent woman, very proud of my heritage. As an individual, knowing who I am and where I come from gives me strength and a sense of peace. It's what drives me to retain and reclaim my right to live life according to the Lord while living in mainstream society. I have forged my own path through self-determination and by reconciling with past wrongs. I face forward now with a knowing, passed onto me from my Elders. I look to my Elders for guidance because they represent the fabric of who we all are, the heart and soul of our culture through time in the dreaming, constant and eternal.

In our culture, a child is more closely related to their maternal grandmother than their parents. This is our kinship and to this day kinship is very strong in Aboriginal society. When I was growing up, I spent more time with my grandparents than I did at home. I was very close to Pop-eye (my grandfather). I adored him and he was beginning to teach me our ways. He died when I was three and a half years old and his death had a huge impact on my life. When I about four or five years old, I cut my fingers using a razor blade, while I was watching Mum sleep. It took me along time to come to terms with losing Pop-eye; in fact it has only been recently that I have grieved properly and moved on. I still had Granny (my grandmother) and I used to go and stay with her in Yarrabah on the Mission. I remember watching her weave baskets and I helped her cook. She used to tell me stories about family, who was who, how we were related and how I was to address them. I loved it at Yarrabah, it was such a paradise. I didn't know it at the time, but we used to have to get a permit before we could visit Granny at Yarrabah. We used to live in a small town called Innisfail, which is an hour's drive south of Yarrabah. Granny came to live with us when she became sick and she died six months later. I was thirteen and suddenly there was no more learning.

I never realised the extent of the fragmentation of our culture until I became aware that it existed in my own family. I always knew I was Aboriginal, but growing up with my Dad's family was very difficult because although we are Aboriginal, we were told to say we are Malay. This bloodline is through Granddad (my Grandfather). I remember I was proud at home, but ashamed and confused in public about my Aboriginality. I went through an identity crisis because I didn't know who I was or where I belonged. I was a lost, confused, very angry and lonely young person. It was only as an adult that I found out that Dad's family identified as Malay publicly out of fear of the children being taken away.

I suffered severe depression and I hated myself. I was starving myself because of this self-hatred. I tried to change to fit in with mainstream society but I always felt like I was on the outside looking in. I was continually subjecting myself to abuse because I thought that I was worthless and a waste of space, who didn't deserve to be here. I was very sick, physically, psychologically, emotionally and spiritually. The very thing that I turned my back on, is my salvation, my family, my culture, my heritage to put it simply, I turned my back on me.

I auditioned at the Aboriginal and Islander Dance Theatre that's based in Sydney. I was accepted and I started to learn about Aboriginal and Islander culture. It was like I was picking up my learning again from when I was thirteen. Learning the traditions of other Aboriginal communities from around the country ignited in me a desire to learn about my culture and my family history. The more I learned and understood, the more self-respect and self-worth I found.

In spite of this, I felt like something was missing and that I wouldn't feel whole until I found it. Dancing helped me to get in touch with my spirituality. I remember the first time I visited Wujal Wujal, Pop-eye's and Granny's mother's home, my ancestral home. I heard them, my ancestors taking to me. I felt the love and the belonging. My picture was taken while I was there sitting on the rock, with the waterfall and the waterhole behind me. My ancestors told me to wash my feet before I departed. This place is my story place.

After visiting home, I had a dream about me swimming there with these two crocodiles. They would circle me and sometimes, I would lay on their backs and dive in the water with them. It was really strange because no one is allowed to swim there because it is sacred. I told one of my granny's about the dream and she asked me if I knew about the legend of that place. I said no, that I didn't, and she told me about a mermaid who swims there with two crocodiles. The crocodiles were in love with the mermaid and then she said to me, you are that mermaid and you are the one, the chosen one. You are the only one who must wash your feet before leaving the area every time you visit.

It doesn't matter where you go this place is in your heart.

Life is no longer a struggle, it is a journey. I am Kuku Yalangi woman and I listen to my Elders for they are guiding me on my journey. My ancestors are back; my grandparents are back because they are alive in me. I know and understand that as long as I live, my culture lives on, for it is eternal. Our ways are always there, be still and listen to the Elders both in the physical world and in the spiritual world and you will hear their words. Reconciling with the past has helped me to heal and move forward. I feel whole now for I have reconnected with love and found harmony.

Youth

Mohawk Translations:

Raronhiena:wi – Name meaning, "He carries the sky."

Kats Ken:a – Come here.

Otkon – The Devil or saying damn.

Sheien:a teiesatonhontso:ni – Your daughter needs you.

Ienonkwatsherenha:wi iesaiats, Okwari nisentaroten, Kanienkehaka nishato:ten – Name "she carries the medicine," you are bear clan, you are Mohawk.

Was onen satorishen iah tehnen onen tesiaien ken:a ne aiesaioten, Nia:wen a:kwe naho:ten nashe:re, was onensasaten:ti – Go home now, rest, you have nothing to do anymore. Thank you for all you have done. Go home now.

Shonkwaiatison – Creator.

Rakeni – Dad. Father.

Reunited Hearts

"Uh, not this song again, HEY Morris change THIS song, we've heard it five times now," yelled the man.

The song was Patsy Cline's, "I Fall to Pieces", and he hated it. No wonder everybody who walked in was depressed and drinking. It's them damn oldies. They're slow and depressing.

"Hey old geezer, shuddup," yelled someone in the background.

"Hey Franky, I'm leaving. See you tomorrow night."

Nelson Miracle was always at the bar, drinking his life away. He had no family; they all abandoned him because he was always drinking. He was never home. His real home was the bar. One day, fifteen years ago, he wasn't surprised to go home, only to find the house bare, as if no one had lived in it. Even the furniture was gone. Wife and kids too, gone, with only crayon marker on the wall saying good-bye. But he didn't care, as long as he had a drink everyday, he didn't care about anything else.

"Bye Nelson," said Franky.

When Nelson got home, his house was a mess as always. Newspapers, magazines, and take-out boxes lay everywhere. Fourteen years worth of dust bunnies coated the furniture. The kitchen was even messier.

"*Raronhienha:wi*," said a really soft voice, that he almost didn't hear.

"*Raronhienha:wi*," a little louder this time.

"Boy, I must really be drunk. Now I'm hearing voices and yesterday it was footsteps." Then suddenly he started to laugh, like what he just said was the funniest thing.

"I'm really drunk. I'm going to bed," he said to himself.

"*Raronhienha:wi kats ken:a.*"

"*Otkon*, I'm fifty-six years old and I still have an overactive imagination." He laughed again.

"*Raronhienha:wi* kats ken:a."

But he ignored it. He went up the stairs to his room. He opened the door and there stood a seven foot women. She had deep black hair that was braided all the way down to her waist. Her skin was the color of dark copper. Her eyes were light brown. She was wearing a beautiful white buckskin dress. A bright light filled his whole room, but the light switch wasn't on. When she spoke her voice sounded like an angel.

"*Sheien:a teiesatonhontso:ni.*"

"What did you say? I don't speak Mohawk." The women looked upset. "Yes, you do. Even though your daughter won't admit it, her heart longs for her daddy's hugs. Your daughter needs you. She needs you beside her, needs to hear your words. Her youngest daughter is dying in front of her, she's dying from an inoperable tumor in her brain. But the doctors are saying she's holding on for some reason, and I know why. It's because your granddaughter wants you and your daughter to reunite," she said.

"But she doesn't even know me, how can she want me and my daughter to reunite?"

"She sees how her mother is sad about losing the only father she has ever loved."

"Is she suffering?" he asked.

"No, she's in a coma; she doesn't feel anything, but she's asking the Creator to hold on long enough to see her mother reunite with her father. That's why I'm here. You're the only person who can make her let go. But she's also scared of going home without knowing who she is. You're the only person that can tell her who she is. Your daughter is scared about how you would feel after no contact in years. Your granddaughter knows all this."

"So you're saying, the person I've been locking up has to resur-

130

face, the person I've been drowning with alcohol, the person who is a loving Grandfather speaking his language and knowing who he is. The person that I don't want to be, has to come back?" he gasped.

"Yes," she said.

He had worked so hard to bury that person he was, the Native man, the man he didn't want to be.

"No, I won't, I won't let that person come back. No!" he yelled. The woman got upset. Through her fingers came something like electricity and on his wall appeared a clear vision. He saw his daughter sitting beside her daughter, her small body still, face pale, a scarf around her head. He clearly saw that his granddaughter looked a lot like him. He saw how beautiful and all grown up his daughter was. But he felt a heavy weight around his heart watching his daughter sitting there holding her small child's hand. She was singing a Mohawk lullaby that he used to sing to his children.

"Okay, I'll go. Where is she staying?"

The next day he was walking down the halls of the hospital, looking for room 5108. When he found the room he hesitated for a moment. But he suddenly heard that song again, which gave him courage to walk in. It was exactly the way he had seen in the vision. Only there was a doctor checking her. He shook his head at the child's mother.

"Nothing's changed, she's still holding on," the doctor said. He looked kind of upset, then walked away.

"My poor baby," she turned to her husband.

"Why, why is she holding on?" Tears ran down her cheeks.

"Um,umh," he said, clearing his throat, "it's because of me."

"*Rakeni*, what are you doing here?"

"She's holding on because she knows how sad you are about leaving fifteen years ago and also for not knowing who she is. She wants to go home knowing who she is. She wants to be able to talk to *Shonkwaiatison*." His daughter looked back at her child, and she cried even more. "I'm so sorry, sorry I never told you who you were. I'm sorry for making you suffer."

"It's my fault too, for never being there for my family, never telling you guys who you were, but, now I'll start." He went over to his granddaughter and took her hand in his.

"*Ienonkwatsherenha:wi iesaiats, Ohkwari nisentaro:ten, Kanienkehaka nishato:ten,*" he started.

"*Was onen, satorishen iah tehen onen tesaien ken:a ne aiesaioten.*

Nia:wen a:kwe naho:ten nasha:re, was onen sasaten:ti" Then suddenly the heart monitor beeped and the line went flat. He saw the woman next to the body of his granddaughter. She was there to take her spirit back to the Creator. She didn't have to say anything, but he knew his granddaughter was grateful for freeing her.

"*O:nen.*" He turned around to hug his daughter, and they cried together for a long time.

After that day he put his drinking days behind him. He now tells stories of the language and culture to all his grandchildren and other children of the community. Both he and his daughter are happy to be back in each other's lives.

Prayer

Let it out
Let it go
Because what has happened
Is not show
I pray for you
As you sit there and cry
Thinking of the facts
Makes me sigh
All my strength
I give to you
To realize
That the tragedy is true
Cry and cry
And let it out
And if you have to
Just scream and shout
Don't feel alone
At any time
Because there is alot of us
Who are very kind
What I have shared
Is just to show that I cared.

Elizabeth Kruger

Us and Stickgame

You are so happy, you are so sweet
You are someone people like to meet

There is a game that binds us as one
Our songs we can sing until the rise of the sun

Our voices together are so loud
That we often attract a very large crowd

One by one we choose the right bones
And sooner or later teams loose their tones

In the end we will win
Because we play fair and never sin

Stickgame is its well known name
And this is what makes us so much the same

Together again we do sing
And make everyones ears ring

We are the champs of this game
And we feel others feeling lame

Different places we do go
Just to have fun and put on a show

Having fun is what we do
And we're always looking for something new

In conclusion I say to you
Something that isn't new

Thank you for being there
Our love and friendship we do share

So if you ever need a friend
My love and wisdom I will send

One more thing I must say too
Is thank you Dolly for being you.

Elizabeth Kruger

When That Day Comes

'Sometimes things happen unexpectedly. People say God works in
mysterious ways, this must be true.'

What happens in life no-one can say
Until they reach that unexpected day

Accepting things that God decides
Is often hard and makes us hurt inside

When that day comes for someone
It's not the choice or fault of anyone

Dealing with that harsh pain
Can make someone go insane

It's so deep and penetrating
Like ripping your body apart
There is no pain as painful as this

What will happen when that day comes
For mothers, fathers, sisters and sons

How can we prepare
For such an awful scare

It hurts just to think about it
I just want to cry and get rid of it

The love we feel for so many
Is so deep, so real, so true
That it would just kill to lose you

I can't change what's going to happen
What will happen, or what won't

All I know is my love for you
Is so deep, so real and so true

And when I do lose you
I will never forget that day
when you told me that you loved me too.

Preston Gregoire

Residential School

You stole me from my family
when I was very young.
When I spoke my own language you
pierced my Native tongue.

I tried to be strong
but instead I cried all night long.
I always felt down.
My smile was a frown.

This is the worst thing I have seen
hoping one night I would wake up from this dream.
If it was long, you would cut my hair.
When I was bad you took my air.
I could see that you had no cares.
Every time I climbed up, you tossed me
back down the stairs.

When something was wrong, I was accused.
I tried to convince but I still got abused.
I got blamed for things I didn't do.
Everything you told me wasn't true.

You always lied.
You told me my family died.
Every time you couldn't find me I took off to pray.
Asking God to bring an end to this day.

When I try to think of the happy times I remember
there was none.
When I ran away all I could do is run.
Remembering every day you fed me gruel.
My feelings spun like a spool.
When I got here the sign said
"Welcome to Residential School."

When I...

When you first met me you
didn't know what to expect,
but you gave me a chance.
You listened when I needed to talk.
You stayed even when I
told you to walk.
So I respect you for that.
I wonder each day why?
You listened and stayed
after I told you off.
It seems like you were
there more than anyone else.
When I wanted to end my life,
you were there.
When I needed to talk,
you were there.
When I wanted to sit in silence,
you sat along with me.
You've seen me shed many tears.
For this you have respect, and a friend.
Cause when I needed a friend
at what seemed to be
the end of my rope,
you came into my life
to be a friend.

One Unlucky Day

On a really unlucky day, an old Native man was walking to the grocery store, which was only two blocks away. He had a blue hat on, the kind all old Native men wear, and a plaid red and green shirt. He was wearing normal jeans and weird work boots. He had a blade of grass in his mouth and was chewing on it constantly. His thumbs were in his two front pockets, making him look as if he had authority.

Just then a teenager on a skateboard came by and knocked the old man over. He fell backwards and his hands flew up in the air. "Oops… sorry old man," the boy had hollered as he skateboarded away. The old man didn't get up, instead he passed out.

"Oh no! Are you okay, old man?" a girl about seven asked him. He started to stand up with her help. He brushed himself off.

"No, I'm not, some punk knocked me over with his skateboard!" and he started to walk away as the little girl followed.

"You should go home to get some rest, because of what happened," the little girl told him. He then smiled at her and replied, "Since when did you have all the knowledge, uh?" and turned around to go home.

"Don't know," she said and the little girl started to giggle. "I'm going to walk with you to make sure nothing bad happens," she told him firmly. He lowered his head and sighed, the younger generations are getting more bizarre by the year.

A few minutes later they arrived at the old man's house. They both entered silently, his house was small, but comfortable. There was no need for him to own a bigger house; it was only himself living in it.

"Okay old man, what's your name?" the little girl asked. He jumped at the question; he almost forgot she was even there.

"Why do you need to know, mmm?" he asked suspiciously. She smiled the grinch smile, because her lips curved way up. "I think it's very important to know who your Elders are, that's why." She said to him sweetly. "My name is George Flayer and before you ask, yes I know my last name sounds a little strange." And he sat down on his chair in the kitchen. She sat in the one across the table.

"Well, I told you mine, now tell me yours." He practically demanded. She smiled sweetly. "I know why people don't respect you." She said. George's eyebrows rose up, "Why?" he asked expecting something insulting. He started to fidget with his fingers. "You don't respect yourself, so how can others respect you." And she started to tap her fingers lightly on the kitchen table. He gave her a look that could kill, and when he usually did this, people usually got the chills. To his surprise she calmed down and took a deep breath. "My name is Sara."

"All Right, Sara, what do you want?" He asked her, getting annoyed now.

"What if I told you I was more than just a little girl?" She asked him. He thought about the question for a few seconds and replied, "I'd say you'd better get help! I can't believe you people of today, you all think you're very important and think we old ones don't know anything…" and he kept saying stuff about how important it is to respect Elders like him.

"ENOUGH!!!" she screamed out loud. She stood up quickly looking down at the very shocked old Native man. "I am a seven hundred year old trapped in a seven year old body." She told him firmly and with such authority that said he shouldn't mess with her. Finally, he got the courage to speak to her. "Well, why are you telling me?" he asked her.

In a cracked voice, "I need to die." She said flatly. She sat back down on the chair and started to tear up. "The worst thing about life is not death, it's living too long when your not supposed to."

George didn't know whether or not to believe her. She's just a little girl, not an old woman. "Why would you want to die?" he asked her, just so he wouldn't make her angry.

"Because I lived too long, way past my time and did things I'm not so proud of." Then she lowered her head so that he couldn't see her face.

"Straight to the point, what do you want me to do about it?" He asked her. She raised her head to face him and gave him a great big smile. "I want you to kill me!" and stood up to open the windows, it was way too hot in the kitchen. He laughed, couldn't help it, but she sounded ridiculous, how can she expect him to kill?

"Sara, I'm no killer, I'm just a crabby old man who gets thrills by looking at the squirrels in my backyard." He thought about it a moment and frowned. "How do I kill you?" She smiled; he was willing to help her out.

"Fire, fire is the only way to kill me." Then she stood up and headed toward the door. "I know what your thinking, why didn't I light myself, right?" He nodded. "No, I can only die if someone else puts me aflame."

"Let's do it right now, that's if you still want to die?" and she smiled.

"You want me gone that quickly?" He nodded and she started roaring with laughter. They then headed outside in his backyard. They were lucky nobody else was outside. George looked at the small little girl; she had blonde hair in pigtails; how cute. He wondered how she came to be this way; it must have been a real bummer to be seven for seven centuries.

He then put gasoline on the little girl. What if she was telling a lie? Would her parents come by to kill him? He was just about to light her aflame when some weird guy in leathers came and took away his matches.

"I don't think so old man! This old lady has to stay alive." Now George got a good look at the weird guy and wished he hadn't. The weird guy had a melted face and his two eyes were different colors. One was black, the other was white. It was a really creepy sight. George had a hard time from saying something bad about his appearance.

"Sara, Sara, tisk, tisk, you know better than to try and escape me!" he told her.

"Hey, you never told me about this guy." George said and Sara smiled weakly. "Um well, he's the one who put the curse on me." Sara looked up at the weird guy to see what he would do.

"The name is, hey I don't see a need to tell you, you're just an old guy" The weird guy turned toward Sara and laughed. "I told you, you'd never die. The same as for the grass; it will always be green and the sky blue."

George noticed a mysterious pouch on the weird man's waist. Without even giving him time to think it through, he ran toward him and stole the pouch. "Hey, you little creep give that back!" and the weird man was after George.

While running, George opened the pouch and poured some of the dust in it on the grass and he muttered Purple. All the grass turned Purple and he said to himself: this must be wishing powder! He tossed some in the air and yelled "Pink" and the whole sky turned pink. "Hey don't mess around with my powder!" The weird man said, but George didn't pay attention to him. He turned toward Sara and said "Dead" and Sara began to die.

"Thank you," Sara said then she turned to ash. He dropped the pouch on the ground and the weird man took it and rewrapped it around his waist. "You idiot! Do you realize what you have done!" and he went up to George and slapped his face. "That's what you get stupid." And he stepped a few feet backward. He put everything back to normal the way it should be. "Now George, it's your turn for trusting little girls that know too much!"

The weird man then took some more powder out of his pouch and threw it on George. "Beetle" and now George is an ugly bug. The weird man picked up the beetle and put him in a glass jar. "You now are my bug, and if you don't behave I'll just squash you, ha ha ha ha ha!"

Then the weird man disappeared along with his beetle and no one ever wondered where the old man named George went. When you're mean and crabby, no one would want to visit and they would never notice that you're gone.

That's the sort of thing that happens on an unlucky day, when you trust little girls with high vocabularies. If you're not careful, it could happen to you!

Vanessa Nelson

Rokstentsherak:sen

One sunny afternoon in Kanehsatake, Hank and his little brother Timmy decide to go for a ride on their bikes. They take the trail to go up Blue Mountain. On their way up they see a big strawberry field in front of a little house, which looks more like a shack than a house.

"Hey Hank, let's take some of those strawberries," little Timmy said.

"But Timmy, that evil old man lives in that house. Haven't you heard about him?" Hank said, shivering in goose bumps.

"You mean Rokstentsherak:sen?"

"Yeah." replied Hank.

"Yeah, I heard about him. He eats children, doesn't he?" little Timmy asked.

"First he watches you pick his strawberries, then he comes out and shoots you with his shotgun. And when you're dead, that's when he takes you in his house and eats you up!" Hank said.

"Yeah right. He's just a crazy old man; he's not going to hurt a little kid like me. You can stay here if you want, but I'm really hungry and I'm going to go pick some strawberries and eat them right on his crappy little porch. Then we'll see if those stories are true," little Timmy said.

"Fine by me, but I don't want to be the one to give your eulogy." Hank says, getting off his bike.

"Eulo-what?" Timmy asks, "Never mind, I'm just going to go have a nice free supper now!" Timmy gets off his bike and walks right into the strawberry patch. He seems a bit hesitant before picking a strawberry, but then grabs all his strength and picks one out of the patch. Hank back at the path covers his face with his hands. Timmy takes the strawberry and it seems like forever before it finally lands in his mouth. He then takes another strawberry and begins walking up towards the porch of the house. At that moment Rokstentsherak:sen comes out of his house with his shotgun and a bottle of beer in the other hand.

"Get the hell outta ma yard you damn kids!" he yells at the kids. Timmy eats the strawberry and then Rokstentsherak:sen takes his shotgun, loads it up with some bullets and then shoots it. Both boys scream like little girls and Hank gets on his bike and bikes away while Timmy falls on the ground and hurts his leg.

"HAAAAAAANK!!!" little Timmy yells, holding his leg. "DON'T LEAVE ME HERE! DON'T LEAVE ME HERE TO DIE!!!!!!!"

Rokstentsherak:sen walks down his porch, accidentally drops his bottle of beer on the ground, and nearly trips and falls.

"Ya damn kids make me drop ma beer. Yar gonna pay!" he yells. He takes his shotgun and points it at Timmy. Timmy screams like a girl as he shoots near him. Timmy crawls behind the strawberry patch, letting his hurt leg drag behind him, and then starts to cry. Rokstentsherak:sen is out of bullets now. He goes towards the patch but then trips on a rock and falls on the ground.

"Are you, are you okay?" little Timmy asks the old man from behind the patch.

"NO, I'VE NEVER BEEN OKAY!" he replies, yelling. Little Timmy walks over to him and then tries to help him up.

"No, no. Get out you damn bugger," Rokstentsherak:sen says, wriggling free of little Timmy's hands.

"But I have to help you, you're an Elder." little Timmy argues. Rokstentsherak:sen gives up arguing and is helped to sit up by Timmy. Timmy sits down on the ground next to him.

"Were you always like this?" Timmy asks, his curiosity getting the better of him.

"Yes." the old man replies.

"Why?"

"Why do you ask so many questions?"

"I just wanna know," Timmy answers.

"Well, I would be down in town more, but I can't speak the language, so they won't give me a job," says Rokstentsherak:sen.

"You can get a job outta town." little Timmy suggests.

"No I can't. The only things I know how to do good is the jobs they have down here. It's useless anyways, look at me. I'm an old man. I can't do anything anymore. People are afraid of me too for some odd reason." Rokstentsherak:sen says, scratching his messy grey hair.

"Oh."

"Yeah. But listen you, you better learn the language. You better keep it going too. You don't want yourself or your future children to suffer, so you better not lose your language. Do it for me, if not for me, do it for yourself and your children," Rokstentsherak:sen says, getting his gun and getting up to walk away.

"Hey! Where you going?" Timmy yells.

"In my house. I've said and done all I could. Now GET off of my property. Timmy listens, getting up and limping all the way to his bike. He takes a quick glance at Rokstentsherak:sen before pedaling back down the mountain.

What Rokstentsherak:sen said that day stuck with Timmy the rest of his life. He learned the language, and taught it to his children, too. And when he heard that Rokstentsherak:sen had passed away, he payed for the funeral and everything else. Few came, but Timmy didn't care, because he knew the real Rokstentsherak:sen, and he wasn't so evil after all.

The End.

Cedar

So strong and tall
You seem all knowing
Can you see where my life
is going?
Do you see my smiles
wipe my tears
know my joys
and calm my fears
You've learned a lot throughout the
years

Joel Morgan

Fire

You wish for more, there is
nothing to hide, that funny
feeling is your fire inside
Burning to be better
flickering for fame
For if you dare get there
your fire will change
From your new knowledge
your flame it will grow
The harder you strive
the more you shall
know

Eagle

Fly towards the sky my friend
do not return or descend
for here on earth life is bad
How can you feel anything but sad
In the sky I see you dance
Why do you give them one
more chance
Look at this earth, it's
slowly dying
but you can't hear it,
It's silently crying

Joel Morgan

Water

Babbling brooks washing clean
the pain and the torments
of yesteryear
They Stole your Culture
Outlawing your song
if it's not just like us, it's got to be wrong
now we have freedom, or so I am told
but the future is endless, who knows
what it holds

Modern Warrior

In the past there has been a certain name given for a person or individual who was chosen specifically by his tribe to carry out certain duties, the special responsibilities that were bestowed upon that certain being has had the privilege of traveling to many distant lands seeing what others only dream of.

These travelers also had specific tasks that must be fulfilled in order to keep his title and honour, these people were our hunters, our scouts for new lands, our protectors, these people were our warriors, they fought to the death for their people.

The day of that reality has now come and gone and now we are to co-exist with many different peoples of race, culture, beliefs, and ethnicity. We as the original descendants to this land have seen many wrongs done to all indigenous peoples of Turtle Island. Lands that have been illegally surrendered, many wrongful deaths and punishments given to the innocent. To this day we still live in that form of oppression. You see it everyday on television, hear it on the radio, and through personal experience. Although it is silent you see it, hear it and most of us have lived through it.

I have experienced this discrimination, racism, prejudice and stereotypes, first hand. It still exists throughout our society, especially in Canada, or should it be called KANATA. You always hear about how great this country is on an international level. The best one to date is, if you're in another country, and you wear a Canadian patch or flag, that you will be treated with the utmost respect.

For what! Is this their greatest accomplishment. It seems to me that the other people use this as an example, like it is their own personal national trophy. I even see other nations, no matter their background, treating all aboriginal people with disrespect, because of the stereotypes that have been bestowed upon our nations. An Indian is an Indian is an Indian, I bet this is another one that all of us hear. In fact it is not, we are not Indians, we are not aboriginals, we are not natives, we are not savages, we are not Bering Strait theory, we are the original people to this land.

Our nations have been here for thousands of years. How else can fifty million people come here, not through migration, that's for sure!

Tell me, can you migrate that many millions, through the harsh elements that the north possesses, it is only common sense that this is an impossibility.

Sure, we are descendants of the Asian people, or are they descendants of us. Remember the super continent theory, see all their teachings starting to work against them.

I, myself, have done nothing wrong to the people that reside on this vast continent, yet I must live and pay for something that I have not purchased. It is a debt that has been brought on through the past two hundred years. My ancestors as well as yours have not known what we are paying for. Yet we must give up all the land, all the resources, all the lost culture, tradition and innocence, all of it surrendered illegally.

It saddens me a great deal to think of what our ancestors have gone through, not only does it make sad, but it is a lingering anger that must be released. An emotion as powerful as that is Love, the love of all indigenous peoples across the globe. There are only a few of us that see the future as well as the past and when the two emotions and time lines are combined it is like a furious passion. A passion to not only live but to succeed in this assimilated lifestyle that has been forcefully given to us, a fury that has been passed down. it is like a gift from the creator that has been given to only the chosen few. The few who dedicate their lives to the modern day battles we are fighting.

I had the opportunity to watch a television program on APTN. This program was about how Christianity has helped aboriginal peoples and one of the gentleman on it had a quote that will always stay in my mind, it was when they came over we had all the land they had the bible, now they have all the land and we have the bible. Well, to me that sucks, pardon the expression. I guess it is my youthful tongue waiting to explode and destroy what I see and hear. That is true and it is also false, you see the influence that our little brother, the white man has brought over is now falling and it is weakening everyday. My dad never had me baptized or taught me about religions, but I did sit through many long pointless hours, days, weeks, and years of lectures by a priest in a church under the catholic religion. Learning their ways but usually thinking of other things and for a good reason, now I understand the will of my dad's intention, and I do have a sense of why I am here in this time line that the creator has granted me.

A long time ago, in the days of our ancestors, we fought amongst each other for land and who knows what, but as I said before those days have come and gone and it is now the future that we as the original peoples must fight for, we must come together, support one another, and be one nation and live the stereotype as, an Indian is an Indian is an Indian.

We will use what they have given to us against their will, we will overcome, and eventually we will succeed without swinging and come out on top. We will use the gifts that the creator has given to us and will live as those special people that our ancestors granted the right to be the fighters and protectors, for we are,
today's Modern Warriors.

Stephanie Lousie Squakin

Tupa (Great Grandmother)

As the warrior stands within
we want to believe in
She's strong and powerful
You see a Native woman, so beautiful.
As pretty as the stars shine above
deep down in a cove
You hear a bear's thunderous roar
You hear a drum beat, you open the door.
You see what lies within,
It's the heart of the brave warrior.
She struggled through her own battle
and won her own wars.
As the eagle stands by watching
She uses his eyes to see far, to catch their next prey.
As the eagle soars the sky
circling up above, he turns shy.
He flies away for just a mere second
he comes back warning her.
There is something coming.
She looks all around,
she finds what he sees, another being.
He wants her to fear.
He thinks of her as helpless as a porcupine.
She digs deep down inside
and finds the strength of wisdom,
voice and control.
He is as ignorant as a pig.
He stands as tall as a rig,
there's no self control.
So she makes herself on patrol.
She uses her knowledge,
her strength,
her power!
But he went to college
went the length

to try to be the perfect flower.
He's rotting inside
She knows his flaws
The warrior wins
her war again
She's the warrior that stands within.

Biographies

A limited edition series of 16' x 20' canvas reproductions of Leonard's above paintings (in full colour) are being offered for sale to help raise funds so he can continue his fight for freedom. For a brochure about these fine art reproductions, please contact: Tate Wikuwa, LLC, 3731 Overland Drive, Lawrence, Kansas, USA 66049-2205

BIOGRAPHY OF LEONARD PELTIER – a father, grandfather, artist, writer, and Indigenous rights activist – is a citizen of the Anishinabe and Dakota/Lakota Nations who has been unjustly imprisoned for nearly twenty-seven years.

A participant in the American Indian Movement, he went to assist the Oglala Lakota people on the Pine Ridge Reservation in the mid-70s where a tragic shoot-out occurred on June 26, 1975. Accused of the murder of two agents of the Federal Bureau of Investigation (FBI), Peltier fled to Canada believing he would never receive a fair trial in the United States. On February 6, 1976, he was apprehended. The FBI knowingly presented the Canadian court with fraudulent affidavits and Peltier was returned to the U.S. for trial. Key witnesses were banned from testifying about FBI misconduct and testimony about the conditions and atmosphere on the Pine Ridge Reservation at the time of the shoot-out was severely restricted.

Important evidence, such as conflicting ballistics reports, were ruled inadmissible. Still, the U.S. Prosecutor failed to produce a single witness who could identify Peltier as the shooter. Instead, the government tied a bullet casing found near the bodies of their agents to the alleged murder weapon, arguing that this gun had been the only one of its kind used during the shootout and that it had belonged to Peltier. Later, Mr. Peltier's attorneys uncovered, in the FBI's own documents, that more than one weapon of the type attributed to Peltier, had been present at the scene and the FBI had intentionally concealed a ballistics report that showed the shell casing could not have come from the alleged murder weapon.

Other troubling information emerged: the agents undoubtedly followed a red pickup truck onto the land where the shoot-out took place, not the red and white van driven by Peltier; and compelling evidence against several other suspects existed and was concealed. At the time, however, the jury was unaware of these facts. Peltier was convicted and sentenced to two consecutive life terms. He is currently imprisoned at the U.S. Penitentiary in Leavenworth, Kansas.

To the international community, Peltier's case is a stain on America's human rights record. Amnesty International considers Peltier a "political prisoner" who should be "immediately and unconditionally released." To many Indigenous peoples, Peltier is a symbol of the abuse and repression they have endured for so long.

BIOGRAPHIES:

AUDREY AVERY is a fifteen year-old Mohawk living in Kanesatake, Quebec. She is now in Secondary 4, attending Ratihente High School.

YVONNE BEAVER – Tuscarora, from the Six Nations Grand River Territory in Ontario. Yvonne was born, raised and received her early education in that community. From her mother came early lessons in the art of story telling. She has a Bachelor of Arts degree in the Social Sciences completed at the University of Western Ontario. She is an active member of the Six Nations Writers group.

LESLEY DAWN BELLEAU is a twenty-six year old Ojibway woman from Garden River First Nation, and currently residing in Toronto, Ontario. She is a graduate from the four year English Literature and Theatre Program of Algoma University in Sault Ste. Marie, working toward a Master's degree in Creative Writing. She is interested in the Native Residential School experience, as her father was a survivor of Garnier School in Spanish, Ontario. She is also a proud mother of my baby boy named Nicolas, who is her source of inspiration and the heart of her existence.

JOHN GARFIELD BARLOW is Mi'kmaq of the Indian Island First Nation in New Brunswick. In his third year student at St. Thomas University, living in Fredericton NB, John lives with his wife April and their son Oegatsa, which means Northern Lights in Mi'kmaq. He has on the David Velezny prize for creative writing the last two years for two short stories titled, *Piggy* and *Buck Fever*.

JOHN D. BERRY – Choctaw/Cherokee/Scots-Irish heritage, Husband, Father, Uncle, MLS, University of Missouri – Columbia MA, Calif. State U. – Fullerton Native American Studies Librarian – Ethnic Studies Library, UC Berkeley. Past President of the American Indian Library Association, 1999-2000. Traditional Stomp Dancer, Oklahoma Native. John is listed on the Native American Authors pages of the Internet Public Library. Many of his poems have been published in print and on the Internet.

BRENT PEACOCK-COHEN is from the Okanagan Nation. He lives on IR 10 in Ashnola, BC. He just finished his Masters in Education from the University of British Columbia. He is currently an instructor at the En'owkin Centre and hopes to start his Ph D soon. His writing attempts to connect tradition to the contemporary.

JULAINE DOKIS of the Ojibway First Nations was born on a rainy spring filled day in May 4th of 1972. She currently resides on Manitoulin Island, Ontario, with her two daughters, Jessica and Dariane. She plans to return to school this fall to study computers.

DARLIEA DOREY is a mother of five children and the grandmother of ten. She has spent the last thirty years working to improve the quality of life for herself, and for Aboriginal people. She has participated on four trips to the United Nations. Three of those being as an official delegate, with the Federal Government of Canada. She has held National positions with Aboriginal Organizations in Ottawa and has continued to focus on social issues facing young Aboriginal single parents. Ms. Dorey is presently working on the completion of a one-hour documentary on Aboriginal Offenders at Springhill Federal Institution.

HELEN-ANNE EMBRY is involved in many volunteer efforts with physically, mentally and terminally ill people, as well as animal causes, environmental efforts, and sustaining the cultures of Métis and Aboriginal peoples.

WILLIAM H. FLOWERS (BILL FLOWERS) was born in Rigolet, Labrador, November 30, 1951. He is a member of the Labrador Inuit Association. Bill graduated from Dalhousie Law School with a Bachelor of Law degree, and articled for the Newfoundland Bar. He currently works with the Atlantic Regional office of the Department of Indian and Northern Affairs and is based in Halifax. His children are Clinton – thirty-two, Jesse – twenty-six, Joey – twenty-two and Allison – nineteen.

GORDON DE FRANE was born in the Chemainus Nation, located on the Central East Coast of Vancouver Island, British Columbia. As a storyteller, he draws upon his family's rich lives as fishers and as saltwater peoples. His stories are informed by Salish teachings. He participated in the Crazy Horse Aboriginal Playwright's Festival in Calgary, 2001. His short story *"Rock Medicine"* was published in the English Course Union's Publication *Chaos*, 2001. He also delivered a paper on the subject of the *"Chosen"* (Two-Spirit People) at the University of Victoria's First People's Symposium, 2001. He currently continues his undergraduate studies at the University of Victoria.

MARCELLE MARIE GAREAU belongs to the Métis Nation. She comes from a family of travelers. People who made their living as they could and where they could. She has done the same and over the years, travelling to many places to earn her living.

RICHARD G. GREEN, author, was born in Ohsweken, in Grand River Territory. He was a columnist for *Turtle Island News* and *Brantford Expositor*. He served as Writer-in-Residence at the New Credit of the Mississauga's First Nation Library. He has instructed Native Studies classes at Mohawk College in Brantford, Ontario, and at Six Nations Polytechnic, Six Nations Reserve. His books include: *The Last Raven* (1994), *The Writing Experience, an Iroquois Guide to Written Storytelling* (2000) and others. He currently resides on the Six Nations Reserve.

ROBERT VINCENT HARRIS is a member of the Sioux Valley Dakota Nation. His first play *Touch* was produced at Brandon University and at the Crazy Horse Aboriginal Playwrights Festival. In 2001, he participated in the Summer Institute of Indigenous Humanities at Brandon University. He was a student at the En'owkin International School of Writing, Indigenous Fine Arts Program.

BARBARA-HELEN HILL, MA is a writer and visual artist residing at Six Nations of the Grand River. She is a Cayuga/Mohawk mother and grandmother of two beautiful grand-daughters. She has just discovered the wonderful medium of fiber arts and is presently working on pieces for a show that she hopes to mount in the next year.

Helen is working to get her published book *Shaking the Rattle – Healing the Trauma of Colonization* reprinted and is also working on a play.

ARNOLD JAMES ISBISTER has been artistic since an early age. He received a scholarship to attend an Art School. In 1975, he attended the International Banff Centre of Fine Arts. In 1976, he enrolled at the University of Saskatchewan in the Bachelor of Fine Arts program, later switching Majors to Psychology. He was employed by the Regional Psychiatric Centre (a federal penitentiary) from 1980-1994. In 1995, he re-established himself as an Artist and was accepted for group exhibitions in SOHO, New York, NY and Nashville, TN.

JAMIE L. JOHN a member of the Kehewin Cree Nation in Alberta, is currently completing his final year at En'owkin International School of Writing. Jamie will be continuing on at The University of Victoria to complete his BFA. He has worked on projects involving film making, directing, and acting. He is a traditional Grass Dancer who has performed and toured. He has also performed Modern Dance. Jamie loves his culture, which shows through in all his performances.

ELIZABETH MARIE KRUGER recently graduated from High School with honours and is now attending College in Spokane, Washington. She plans to excel in Computer Sciences and move on to Engineering. She is eighteen years old and is part of the Okanagan Nation, and a member of the Penticton Indian Band. She has been writing poetry for several years but never tried to publish her poems. She hopes to one day get a book published, composed of all her poetry.

ROXANNE LINDLEY is a member of the Westbank First Nation in the interior of British Columbia.

ANITA LOUIE is part of the Okanagan Nation located on the Penticton Indian Band Reserve. She is twenty years old and a graduate of Penticton Secondary School. She has lived on the Penticton Indian Band Reserve for most of her life. She is the youngest in her family with an older brother and an older sister.

MENA MAC (TRACY MCCARTHY) is an Aboriginal (Kuku Yalangi) writer and has been writing for ten years. She has written mainly poetry and recently completed a fairytale called '*The Magic Serpents*', a creation story based on the rainbow serpent. This is the first book in a series of four. Mena has also written a trilogy which includes: *Mookai:* (Mookai means grandmother in Mena's language) the life story of her grandmother and great grandmother, *The Winds of Heaven*: Looking at the lives of four Aboriginal women and how they forged careers in the face of adversity, and *From the Heart of a Fringe Dweller*: an autobiography about Mena's spiritual journey.

VERA MANUEL is Secwepemc and Ktunaxa from the interior of British Columbia. She is a storyteller, poet, playwright and co-founder of Storyteller Productions which produces plays and other creative processes for addressing issues and challenges faced by First Nations communities. Published materials include a play titled *Strength of Indian Women*, *Gatherings 11* and others. Vera has recently written and produced a play titled *Every Warrior's Song*.

MAXINE MATILPI is a member of the Kwakiutl Nation whose territory is on Northern Vancouver Island. She works as a lawyer and is the Chief Negotiator for the Kwakiutl Nation. She also teaches First Nations Women's Studies at Malaspina University College. Her other published works include *Shortbread and Ooligan Grease* and *Aboriginal Women and the Law: Colonial History/Current Reality.* She has three sons and lives on Vancouver Island.

MINNIE MATOUSH is from the Cree Nation of Mistissini Lake, Northern Quebec, and acknowledges her ancestry from two First Nations of northern Quebec, Cree-Naskapi and Montagnais descent. She grew up in Mistissini Lake, and takes pride in being able to speak her mother tongue, Cree. Currently she works as a social counsellor at Cree School Board, Post Secondary Student Services in Hull, PQ. She is enrolled in a Masters in Education at Ottawa U., doing her concentration on Career Counselling. She is a single mother of two. Her son and daughter are in High School.

CHARLOTTE MEARNS is from Musqueam First Nation. Charlotte has dedicated her career toward Aboriginal justice services and programming in British Columbia, and recently has been involved in the regional administration (with Lu'ma Native Housing Society as the host agency) for the Government of Canada's National Homelessness Strategy.

KAWENNENHAWI NELSON is a fifteen year old status Mohawk from Kanehsatake, Quebec. She is in Grade Nine at the Ratihen:te High School in Kanehsatake. Kawennenhawi is fluent in Mohawk and proficient in English and French. In 2001, she was awarded the "Aboriginal Youth" Bursary of $750 from FAAY (Foundation For The Advancement of Aboriginal Youth). Her goals are to either study medicine or become a teacher of the Mohawk language.

VANESSA NELSON is a Mohawk from Kanehsatake in Quebec. She is currently attending Ratihen:te High School. She is fifteen years old and was published in *Gatherings 11* in 2000. She is thinking about writing a novel.

VERA NEWMAN is an Elder from the Namgis First Nation in Alert Bay, BC.

RICHARD O'HALLORAN is an Aboriginal who is very interested in becoming a published poet/author. He is a Mohawk born to Wahta Territory in Muskoka, Ontario. He began to write at the age of nine and has been using it as a passive form of coping ever since. He used to write of usually negative issues because that is what he was going through at the time, but has recently changed to more guiding forms of positive affirmation.

DAWNA ELAINE PAGE (KARONHIAKWAS) is a mixed-blood member of the Mohawk Nation at Akwesasne, living with her husband and three children near Chicago, Illinois. She hears the stories of her people crying out to be told, and does her best to capture their words.

JANET MARIE ROGERS has returned to her place of birth, British Columbia after growing up in her father's ancestral territory of the Six Nations Reserve in southern Ontario. Janet has several self-published chap-books, and has other published works in a variety of genres. She performs some of her literary pieces as spoken word and performance poetry. She has received invitations to perform her poetry in cities such as New York, Washington D.C. Wellington N.Z. and Toronto just to name a few. She works as a First Nations Support worker with a school district in Victoria B.C.

DAWN M. RUSSELL is currently walking Mother Earth as a member of the *Syilx* Nation, Penticton Indian Band. A single mother of one and employed with the Surrey School District as an Aboriginal Support Worker; Dawn spends most of her time and energy being a positive role model to all those she meets.

STEVE RUSSELL is a citizen of the Cherokee Nation of Oklahoma. He is an Associate Professor of Criminal Justice, Indiana University at Bloomington. He is a retired judge, past President of the Texas Indian Bar Association, and a member of the Native Writers Circle of the Americas and the Wordcraft Circle of Native Writers and Storytellers.

STEPHANIE LOUISE SQUAKIN is a member of the Lower Similkameen Indian Band of the Okanagan Nation. She is presently working as a summer student on a environmental renewal project. Stephanie will continue her education in the fall, taking a Long Term Care course, which helps her to take care of the elderly in her community.

REBEKA TABOBONDUNG is a member of the Wasauksing First Nation. She is a video documentary maker, poet, and dedicated community activist, her works are provocative. Rebeka has traveled extensively through Central America working to build meaningful links between North and South Indigenous Nations.

DREW HAYDEN TAYLOR is Ojibway from Ontario's Curve Lake First Nations. He is an award winning playwright, journalist and author of 13 books, including three books in the humorous *Funny You*

Don't Look Like One series. He has written television scripts for *The Beachcombers, North of 60, Street Legal and The Longhouse Tales.* Other avenues of expression include a regular column in three Canadian newspapers (as well as frequent articles in numerous magazines) and the director of the film *Redskins, Tricksters and Puppy Stew*, a documentary on Native humor from the National Film Board of Canada.

NAOMI WALSER belongs to the Beausoliel Band from Christian Island. She is a twenty-five year old Aboriginal woman, currently enrolled in an Aboriginal Studies program at Langara C.C. She has had the fortune of travelling around the world playing for the Canadian Field Lacrosse Team. Through the years she has discovered that the sky really is the limit!

ADDITIONAL CONTRIBUTORS: Preston Gregoire, Joel Morgan, Eric Ostrowidzki and Karen Pheasant.